I0639481

Samuel Richardson

The History of Sir Charles Grandison

Samuel Richardson

The History of Sir Charles Grandison

ISBN/EAN: 9783743400382

Manufactured in Europe, USA, Canada, Australia, Japa

Cover: Foto ©Raphael Reischuk / pixelio.de

Manufactured and distributed by brebook publishing software
(www.brebook.com)

Samuel Richardson

The History of Sir Charles Grandison

THE HISTORY

OF

Sir Charles Grandifon.

Abridged from the Works of

SAMUEL RICHARDSON, Efq.

Author of PAMELA and CLARISSA.

The Firſt BOSTON EDITION, adorned with CUTS.

BOSTON:

Printed and ſold by SAMUEL HALL, No. 53, Cornhill.
1794.

THE
HISTORY
OF
Sir CHARLES GRANDISON.

CHAP. I.

A concise Account of Sir Thomas Grandison and his Lady, and the Education they gave their Son. The Death of that Lady.

SIR CHARLES, the fubject of this Hiftory, was the only fon of Sir Thomas Grandifon, a perfon fond of magnificence and fplendor, who valued himfelf on his breed of race-horfes and hunters, and on his kennels, in which he was prodigioufly extravagant. He inherited from his father an eftate in England, which brought in 6000 *l.* a year, and another in Ireland, worth about 2000 *l.* per annum, befides a very confiderable fortune in money. His lady, who was of a noble family, alfo brought him a great fortune. She was a moft excellent woman, to whom he was a complaifant, but carelefs hufband. Soon after his marriage, giving way to his predominant inclination for pleafure, he entirely left the care of the family to her, who cheerfully applied herfelf

to the domeſtic duties; and finding that ſhe could not
prevail on Sir Thomas to reduce his expences, ſhe thought
it prudent to uſe her utmoſt endeavours to enable him
to ſupport them, without diſcredit to himſelf, or any
viſible injury to his family. Yet this lady, while ſhe uſed
the beſt œconomy, was free from all narrow, mean, and
ſelfiſh views : ſhe was beloved for her benevolence and
generoſity, and idolized by her poor neighbours. She had
a plentiful table, and was extremely hoſpitable, both from
her natural goodneſs, and to give credit to her huſband.
By this excellent lady, Sir Thomas had a ſon and two
daughters, who received from her the beſt part of their
education, ſhe inſtilling into their young minds the firſt
principles of chriſtianity, and ſtrong ideas of moral rectitude.

Sir Thomas, conſidering his daughters as an incum-
brance, grew exceſſively fond of his ſon, and placing all
his affections on him, was deſirous of his becoming
maſter of every accompliſhment : he early filled his mind
with high notions of honour, and before he had reached
his thirteenth year, provided him a maſter to inſtruct
him in the ſcience of defence ; hence the amiable youth
ſoon acquired ſuch ſkill in the weapons, as gave the greateſt ſatisfaction both to his father and maſter. He had
remarkable ſtrength of body, with great agility, and
this exerciſe added to both, while the praiſes he received from his father and maſter ſo inflamed his
courage, that he was almoſt tempted to wiſh for a
ſubject to exerciſe it upon. His excellent mother, however, trembled for the effects of their praiſes, which ſhe
dreaded might render him too liable to take offence, and
to reſent it with the ſword, to the danger of his own life,
or of his future peace of mind ; and was continually diſ-

courfing to him on the virtues of true magnanimity, the law of kindnefs, benevolence, and forgivenefs of injuries; frequently reminding him, that what he was then learning was called the fcience of defence, and not of offence.

Mr. Grandifon had the misfortune to lofe this beft of mothers while young ; but it was by a circumftance that deeply impreffed all her leffons on his heart. His father was brought home, as it was thought, mortally wounded in a duel, when this good lady's furprife threw her into fits, from which fhe was never after free, and the danger in which Sir Thomas continued for a confiderable time, with her extraordinary folicitude and care in attending him night and day, broke her conftitution, and brought her into an ill ftate of health, that foon proved fatal. A few hours before this excellent lady expired, after having, on general principles, warmly recommended to her children, duty to their father, and brotherly and fifterly love, as neceffary to their happinefs, fhe had a private difcourfe with her fon on the fame fubject, in which fhe with great affection recommended his fifters to him : they entering at this inftant found him in tears, when the amiable youth, taking each of their hands, kneeled down, and put them into his mother's held-out dying hand ; then bowing his face upon all three, he cried, All, madam—all, my deareft, beft of mamma's, that you have enjoined—He was unable to proceed ; but their arms were bedewed with his tears. ——Enough, enough, my fon, I diftrafs you ! fhe returned, and kiffing her own arm, added, Thefe, my dear, are precious tears—you embalm me with your tears,——O how precious the balm ! Then lifting up her head, fhe kiffed him, and repeated her bleffings. '

Upon her death, the engaging youth became inconfolable. He loved his father, but had been more particularly fond of his mother. Sir Thomas, though he had given but little attention to his education in general, was extremely fond of him, and had taken the lefs care on this head, as he was well convinced that his negleĉt would be well fupplied by his excellent lady, who had mingled her inftruĉtions with thofe of the mafters of the feveral fciences, who, at her defire, attended upon him.

CHAP. II.

Mr. Grandifon *fets out on his Travels. The diffolute Life of* Creutzer, *his Governor. Mr.* Grandifon *becomes intimate with Dr.* Bartlett, *Governor to* Lorimer, *a profligate young Gentleman, who contracts an Intimacy with* Creutzer, *the latter commits Crimes which oblige him to feek his Safety in Flight. Mr.* Lorimer *and a Courtezan confpire the Death of Dr.* Bartlett ; *which is near being effected. Mr.* Lorimer'*s Death. Inftances of Mr.* Grandifon'*s Generofity.*

THE young gentleman being feized with a deep melancholy on his fuffering fo irreparable a lofs, his father, who was alfo greatly grieved, and the more fo, as he could not help reproaching himfelf for having, in fome meafure, been the occafion of that lofs, yielded to the entreaties of General W. his late lady's brother, to permit him to travel. The general recommended for a governor to Mr. Grandifon, one Creutzer, an officer under him, who having been wounded, was obliged to quit the army. Sir Thomas allowed his fon, who

was about feventeen, 800l. a year, from the time of his
fetting out on his travels, and fometime after raifed his
allowance to 1000l.

Creutzer, though recommended by his uncle, foon
convinced Mr. Grandifon, that he was a moft abandoned profligate ; he had, however, the happinefs, by his
prudence, to efcape feveral fnares which this artful wretch
laid for his virtue, from the hopes, that if he could betray
him into them, he fhould filence his remonftrances a-
gainft his own bad conduct, and prevent his complaining
of him in his letters to Sir Thomas.

When they were at Turin, Mr. Grandifon commenced
an acquaintance with Dr. Bartlett, governor to Mr. Lorimer, a young gentleman, with whom Mr. Creutzer became extremely intimate, and the two former became as
clofely united from their good qualities, as the two latter
from their bad ones. Several riotous things were done
there by Mr. Grandifon's governor and Lorimer,
who, notwithftanding the Doctor's ufing his utmoft endeavours to keep them afunder, were almoft conftantly
together ; but one of their exploits rendering them in
danger from the civil magiftrate, Creutzer, to avoid the
punifhment he deferved, fled to Rome, from whence he
wrote to defire Mr. Grandifon to join him in that city.

The worthy youth, who had often in vain threatened
to complain of him to his father, then fent to inform him
of the profligacy and abandoned principles of the man
who had been placed over him, in order to direct his conduct, and to intreat him to appoint him another govern-
or, or permit him to return to England, till he had chofe
one for him. In the mean time he befought Doctor
Bartlett to allow him to apply to him for his advice and

inftruation, till he had received his father's anfwer. Sir
Thomas wrote him word, that having heard of his prudence from every mouth, he gave him full liberty to
choofe what companion he pleafed, and appointed him
no other governor but his own difcretion. Upon this,
Mr. Grandifon, more earneftly than before, with a modefty and diffidence of himfelf, fuited to his natural generofity of temper, that would never permit him to grow
vain, and affuming upon indulgence, entreated the Doctor's directions with the greateft earneftnefs ; and when
they were obliged to part, they eftablifhed a correfpondence that was to laft as long as their lives.

While the empty and profligate Mr. Lorimer paffed through a few of the cities of Lombardy, where he
fpent his time in diffipation, and attending the idle diverfions of the places in which he lived, Mr. Grandifon
made almoft the tour of Europe, and yet took fufficient
time to make fuch remarks upon perfons, places, and
things, as could fcarcely be believed to be the obfervations of a man fo young.

Dr. Bartlett obferving the idle manner in which Mr.
Lorimer fpent his time, was the more patient, as he hoped
the carnival at Venice would be over before his pupil
got to that city. But Lorimer fufpecting that he intended to prevent his being there, gave his governor the flip,
and got thither at the very begining of it. The Doctor
was obliged to follow him, and on his arrival at Venice,
had the mortification to hear that he was one of the moft
diffolute perfons there. When he faw him again, he fet
before him the example of Mr. Grandifon, a much
younger man, and endeavoured to infpire him with emu-
lation, by reading to him fome of Mr. Grandifon's let-

ters. But all the effect thefe had upon him, was to en-
creafe his averfion both to his governor and to that gentleman. However, by one of thefe letters, he for a time
obtained fome reputation : it was written fome months
before it was fhewn him, and defcribed fome places of note
through which Mr. Grandifon had paffed ; he therefore
contrived to fteal it, and his father having frequently defired him to let him fee a fpecimen of his obfervations on
his travels, he copied it almoft verbatim, and fent it as
his own. The Doctor was greatly furprifed on his receiving a congratulatory letter from his father on
his fon's improvements, mixed with fome little afperity
at the Doctor's having reprefented him in a too difadvan-
tageous light. The fond father obferved, that he could
never believe that a fon of his wanted genius, and he
was certain he needed nothing but to apply. He then
gave orders for doubling the value of his next remittance.
Upon this, Doctor Bartlett taking the young gentleman
to tafk, he owned what he had done, and feemed greatly
elated at his contrivance. His governor, however,
thought proper to undeceive the father. Mr. Lorimer,
enraged at Doctor Bartlett for expofing him, and for his
continually obftructing his lawlefs purfuits, was determined to make him repent it ; and becoming ～～～～～
with a courtezan, who by her fubtle and ～～～～～
trivances had ruined many young travellers, they joined
in a refolution to be revenged on the Doctor, whom they
confidered as their greateft enemy. They formed feveral projects, and one of them proved fo fuccefsful, as
to put his life in the greateft danger. Great pains
had been taken with Lorimer to inftruct him in the
hiftories of ancient Greece and Rome ; and his tutor
being a learned man, was very defirous of feeing thofe

B

places of ancient Greece of which he had read fo much. Doctor Bartlett, with great difficulty, prevailed on the young man to leave Venice, where the vile woman, and the diverfions of the place, had taken fcandalous hold of him. He took him with him to Athens, where he at length found that very woman, who had given him fuch uneafinefs at Venice, had followed them, and was ftill Lorimer's miftrefs. However, upon their being guilty of fome frefh enormities, he complained of her to the tribunal of Chriftians, confifting of eight venerable men, out of the eight divifions of the city, who determine caufes among the Chriftians; when, they taking cognizance of the facts, this abandoned woman fuborned wretches to accufe the Doctor to the Cadi, who is the Turkifh judge of the place, as a dangerous, difaffected perfon : and he being corrupted by prefents, got the Vayvode or governor to interfere, on which the Doctor was feized, and thrown into prifon. His Chriftian friends in the place were forbidden to interpofe in his favour. He was denied the ufe of pen and ink, and all accefs to him was prohibited. After which, the vile woman, having taken proper meafures with the perfons fhe had fuborned for continuing the worthy Doctor in his fevere confinement, returned with her paramour to Venice, where they abandoned themfelves to the moft diffolute manner of life.

In the mean time, Mr. Beauchamp, a young man of learning and fine parts, who had fome time before made an acquaintance with Mr. Grandifon, vifiting Athens, was informed of the Doctor's misfortune, and being told that Mr. Grandifon was then at Conftantinople, fent a man on purpofe to inform him of the whole affair, with all the particulars that had come to his knowledge. Mr. Grandifon, who, at this information, was ftruck with grief and aſtoniſhment, immediately applied to the Engliſh Ambaſſador at the Porte, and alſo to the French Miniſter there, to whom he was known, and they made application to the grand Vizier ; upon which an order was iſſued for ſetting the Doćtor at liberty. Mr. Grandiſon, with a view to haſten the Chiaux who carried it, accompanied him, and reached Athens juſt as the Vayvode, who had found the Doćtor's finances exhauſted, had determined to get rid of the whole affair in a private manner by the bowſtring. The danger endeared the Doćtor to the generous mind of Mr. Grandiſon ; and ſo happy and ſenſible a relief endeared Mr. Grandiſon to the Doćtor ; while both of them were filled with gratitude to Mr. Beauchamp, who had buſied himſelf in the beſt manner he could to ſuſpend the fatal blow, and would not leave Athens till he had ſeen the Doćtor delivered.

Mr. Lorimer's father not having the leaſt idea that his ſon had any concern in the plot formed againſt Doctor Bartlett, wrote to entreat that gentleman, when he had obtained his liberty, to take his ſon again under his care ; and the Doćtor, as little thinking then that his pupil had been capable of ſo baſe an inſtance of villainy, returned to Venice, and got him out of the hands of the vile woman, after which they went to Rome. But there the unhappy Lorimer, continuing his profligate courſes, at length became a ſacrifice to his vices. On his death-bed, he confeſſed his connivance at the plots which this infamous woman had formed againſt the Doćtor, and particularly that which ſhe had carried into execution at Athens. He was filled with horrors not to be deſcribed, and as his death approached, begged for life with the greateſt earneſtneſs, promiſing, on that condition, the moſt perfećt reformation. The manner of his death, and the crimes of which he confeffed himfelf guilty, by the inftigation of the moft abandoned of women, fo fhocked and afflicted his governor, that he fell ill.

In the mean while, Mr. Grandifon vifited feveral parts of Afia and Africa, and in particular Egypt, during which he carried on a correfpondence with Doctor Bartlett. On his return to Italy, and joining his two friends, he engaged the Doctor to accompany Mr. Beauchamp into fome of the eaftern regions, which he himfelf had been particularly pleafed with, and, as he faid, wanted to be more exactly informed of ; and therefore infifted on its being undertaken at his own expence ; for he knew that Mr. Beauchamp had a ftep-mother, who had prevailed on his father to take off two thirds of the allowance he made him when he fet out on his travels.

That gentleman was very unwilling to comply with the condition impofed on him by his beloved friend ; but Mr. Grandifon was never at a lofs for arguments to keep thofe in countenance whofe intereft he promoted, and to make their acceptance of his favours appear to be both a duty and an obligation conferred on himfelf. Indeed, Mr. Grandifon delighted in doing good. Thus, while he was at Leghorn, where he refided fometime for the conveniency of the Englifh chapel, he lent an honeft tradefman a confiderable fum on his bond ; but after a while, things not anfwering the poor man's expectation, that benevolent young gentleman took notice that he feemed dejected, and occafionally came into his company with' fuch a fenfe of obligation in his behaviour and countenance, as filled him with compaffion. Why, faid he to himfelf, fhould I keep it in my power to diftrefs one, whofe modefty and diffidence fhews that he deferves

to be made eafy ? My life is uncertain ; I may die fuddenly ; my executors may think it but juftice to exaƈt
payment, and that may involve the poor man in as great
difficulties as thofe from which this money has delivered
him. I will therefore make his heart light, and inftead
of fuffering him to figh over his uncertain profpeƈts at
his board or in his bed, I will make both eafy to him.
His wife and children fhall rejoice with him ; they fhall
fee his countenance again fhine upon them, and occafionally meet mine with grateful comfort. He then can-
celled the bond ; and at the fame time, fearing that the
poor man's diftrefs might be deeper than he was willing to
acknowledge, offered to lend him a farther fum. But by
his behaviour upon this generous offer, he found that the
fum he owed, and his doubts of being able to pay it in
time, were his only grievances ; for he gratefully declined
the additional offer, and from that time walked ereƈt
with a cheerful countenance.

CHAP. III.

An Account of a noble Family at Bologna. *Mr.* Grandifon's *Friendſhip for Seignier* Jeronymo, *whom he in
vain endeavours to reform.   They quarrel ;   Mr.
Grandifon refuſes to draw his Sword ;   but afterwards
ſaves his Life.   The Gratitude ſhewn by all* Jeronymo's
Family on this Occaſion.

WE are now going to enter on many intereſting
ſcenes ariſing from Mr. Grandifon's connections
with perſons who from henceforward will make a very
conſiderable figure in this hiſtory, and with whom it is
neceſſary to render the reader acquainted.

At the city of Bologna, and in the neighbourhood of
Urbino, are two branches of a noble family, who are
Marquiſſes and Counts of Porretta, and trace their pedi-
gree from the Roman Princes.   In Bologna is the Mar-
cheſe della Porretta, a nobleman of diſtinguiſhed merit,
whoſe lady is illuſtrious for her deſcent, her prudence,
her goodneſs of heart, and ſweetneſs of temper.   They
have three ſons and a daughter.   The eldeſt of the ſons
is a general officer in the ſervice of the king of the Two
Sicilies, and is a man of great honour and diſtinguiſhed
bravery, but being proud of his deſcent, is haughty and
paſſionate.   The ſecond, who belongs to the church, is
already a biſhop.   The third, who is called Seignior Jeronymo, and ſometimes the Barone della Porretta, has a
regiment in the king of Sardinia's ſervice.   The ſiſter is

beloved by them all; she has a fine person, is gentle in
her manners, and has lofty, but just notions of the honour of her sex : she is pious, beneficent, and charitable.

The ingenious and engaging Mr. Grandison became
intimate with Seignior Jeronymo while at Rome. This
youth had many fine qualities ; he had such a sweetness
of manners, and was so delighfully gay and lively, that
every one sought for his company ; but he unhappily had
a set of dissolute companions, with whom he was very de-
sirous of bringing Mr. Grandison acquainted.   That
gentleman suffered himself several times to be brought
into their company ; but as he found they were totally
abandoned in their morals, he earnestly endeavoured to
draw his friend from such dangerous companions, by op-
posing their libertine principles ; but infatuated by a love
of pleasure, he had not the courage to forsake them, or to
resist their attacks upon his morals.   However, Mr.
Grandison's friendship was so sincere as to induce him to
make use of all his abilities to reclaim him ; but finding
his repeated admonitions were to no purpose, he had re-
course to writing, and sent him a friendly and affectionate letter, in which he exposed the weakness of the arguments used by his libertine companions, and in a forcible
manner represented the motives to virtue and honour,
and the meanness which is the inseparable companion of
guilt.   Let us consider, said he, the object of your pur-
suit.   Are they women you have seduced from the path
of virtue, who would, perhaps, have otherwise married,
and made useful members of society ? What a capital
crime is a seduction of this kind ! Can you glory in the
virtue of your own sister, and allow yourself to destroy
the virtue of the daughter or the sister of another ? Men,
in the pride of their hearts, are apt to suppose that nature

has defigned them to be fuperior to women. The higheft proof that can be given of fuch fuperiority, is the protection afforded by the ftronger to the weaker; but what can he fay for himfelf and his proud pretenfions, who employs all his art to feduce, betray, and ruin her whom he ought to guide and protect ?—Sedulous to fave her, perhaps, from every foe but the devil and himfelf.

What a bleffing are good children to their parents ! but what comfort can that parent have in children born the heirs of difgrace, and who, owing their very being to profligate principles, have no family honour to fupport, no fair example to imitate, but muft be warned by their father, when he is convinced by bitter experience, to fhun the paths he has trod ? On the other hand, how delightful is the domeftic connection ! to bring to the paternal and fraternal dwellings, a fifter, a daughter, that fhall be received with tender love, to ftrengthen your own intereft by an alliance with fome noble and worthy family, who fhall rejoice to truft to the Barone della Porretta the darling of their hopes !—This would, to a generous heart like yours, be the fource of infinite delights. But could you now think of introducing to the friend you revere, the unhappy object of a vagrant affection ? Muft not my Jeronymo eftrange himfelf from his home, to conceal from his father, from his mother, from his fifter, perfons fhut out from their fociety by all the laws of honour ? Juftly do you boaft of the nobility of your defcent, of the excellence of every branch of your family. Bear with my queftion, my Lord, Are you determined to fit down with the honour of your anceftors ? Your progenitors, and every one of your own family, have given you reafon to applaud their worth : will you not give them caufe to boaft of yours ? You have fhewed me letters from your noble father, from your mother, from the pious prelate your brother, and ftill, if poffible, more admirable ones from your fifter, all filled with concern for your prefent and future welfare. How dearly is my Jeronymo beloved by his whole family, and how tenderly does he love them ! What ought to be the refult ? Jeronymo cannot be ungrateful. He knows fo well what belongs to the character of a dutiful fon and an affectionate brother, that I need not attempt to enforce their arguments.

The Barone had a high fpirit, and could not bear to be oppofed in any purfuit in which his paffions were engaged : hence he was difpleafed at the generous freedom of this letter, and Mr. Grandifon foon became lefs folicitous to cultivate a friendfhip with a perfon, who, where his morals were concerned, could not bear the moft friendly admonitions. They therefore feparated, and during their abfence dropped all correfpondence with each other. The Barone, however, being fome time after involved by his libertine companions in great difficulties, broke his connection with them, and afterwards accidentally meeting Mr. Grandifon at Padua, their friendfhip was again renewed at the earneft defire of Jeronymo. That youth thought himfelf reformed, and Mr. Grandifon flattered himfelf that his reformation was real ; but in a little time he met with a temptation which he had not the refolution to refift. This was from a lady more famed for her birth, her beauty and fortune, than for her prudence and virtue. Before Jeronymo became acquainted with her, fhe had fpread her fnares for Mr. Grandifon, and being exafperated at his flighting the ad-

vances fhe had made him, fhe hoped now to find an opportunity of being revenged.

Mr. Grandifon, being deeply concerned at the infatu-
ation of his friend, thought himfelf under an obligation,
both from honour and confcience, to endeavour, by writing him another letter, to recal him to the paths of virtue.
He, in the gentleft and moft friendly terms, cenfured his
conduct, and ftrove to put him on his guard, by informing him that his life was in danger from two men of violent tempers, who, unknown to each other, confidered
this lady as their own. Jeronymo was fo weak as to let
her fee the contents of this letter ; he even refolved to
vindicate her honour, and prompted by this revengeful
woman, defired, and challenged his friend. Mr. Grandifon, with a noble difdain, refufing to draw his fword,
appealed to Jeronymo's cool reflections ; high words arofe
between them ; Jeronymo even called him coward ; but
Mr. Grandifon, after a violent ftruggle with himfelf,
maftered his temper, and defying the unjuft cenfures of
the world, told him that he would never meet as a foe
the man he had ever defired to confider as his friend. If
ever we meet again, I affure you, he added, it muft be
by accident ; and then it will be time enough to difpute
the occafion of this mifunderftanding. Indeed, the next
meeting was unfought for. Jeronymo rafhly purfuing
the adventure, which had occafioned this mifunderftanding, one of the lady's admirers hired feveral Brefcian
bravoes to affaffinate him. They made their attempt in
the Cremonefe, where they fell upon him, in a thicket
at a diftance from the road.

Happily Mr. Grandifon was paffing by, attended by
two fervants, when a frighted horfe, with his bridle

broke, and his faddle bloody, ran acrofs the way. Mr.
Grandifon imagining that fome mifchief had befallen the
rider, drove down the opening from which the horfe
came, and foon beheld a man ftruggling on the ground
with two ruffians, one ftopping his mouth, and the other
ftabbing him. Mr. Grandifon then jumped out of the
poft-chaife, drew his fword, and ran towards them as faft
as he was able, calling to his fervants to follow him. On
this the villains fled, when he heard one of them fay, Let
us make off, we have done his bufinefs. Shocked at the
villainy of thefe affaffins, he purfued and came up with
one of them, who turning upon him, he beat down the
fellow's blunderbufs at the inftant he prefented it at him,
then wounded and threw him on the ground ; but obferving the other ruffian turning back to help his companion, and two others fuddenly appearing with their horfes,
he thought it more prudent to make his retreat, though
he was very defirous of fecuring one of them. His fervants, at the fame inftant feeing his danger, hafted
fhouting towards him, when the bravo's, perhaps, imagining there were more ftill behind, feemed as glad to efcape with their refcued companion as he was to leave
them. Mr. Grandifon then hafted to the unhappy man ;
but how great was his aftonifhment, when he found him
to be Jeronymo, who had been purfuing his amour in
difguife !

As he gave figns of life, Mr. Grandifon immediately
fent one of the fervants to Cremona for a furgeon, and
in the mean while bound up two of his wounds, one in
his breaft, and the other in his fhoulder ; but he had another in his hip, which his young deliverer found beyond
his fkill to manage : he however ftrove to ftop the blood

C

with his handkerchief, and having lifted him into his
chaife, ftepped in with him, and held him up in it, till
he was told by one of his men, that in another part of
the thicket he had found the Barone della Porretta's fervant bound and wounded, and near him his horfe lying
dead. At this Mr. Grandifon ftepped out, and finding
the poor fellow faint with his wounds, and unable to ftand,
put him into the chaife ; then walked by its fide, and in
this manner moved flowly towards Cremona, in order to
fhorten the way of the expected furgeon, who foon met
them.

The poft-chaife was ftopped, when the furgeon entering it, found that the Barone had fainted away ; but he
dreffed his wounds, and proceeded with him to Cremona :
where opening his eyes, he beheld and knew Mr. Grandifon ;
and being informed by the furgeon that he owed his life
to him, O Grandifon, faid he, that I had followed your
advice ! that I had kept my promife with you !——How
did I infult you !——Can my generous deliverer forgive
me ? If it pleafe God to reftore me, you fhall be the
guide of my future life.

Mr. Grandifon ftaid with him till he was fit to be removed from Cremona, where he was vifited by his whole
family. Never was there a family more affectionate to
each other ; for the fuffering of one was the fuffering of
all. The Barone was extremely beloved by his father,
mother, and fifter, for his affectionate heart, and the engaging fweetnefs of his manners. It is therefore eafy to
conceive how acceptable to the whole family was the important fervice which Mr. Grandifon was fo happy as to
render their Jeronymo. They all joined in bleffing him,
which they repeated with double ardour when they knew

that he was the perfon whom their Jeronymo, during
their intimacy, had warmly extolled in his letters to both
his brothers and to his fifter, and who now told them the
occafion of their quarrel, with circumftanoes as much to
Mr. Grandifon's honour as they were difgraceful to himfelf.   While his generous friend attended him by his
bed's fide, he frequently called for a repetition of thofe
arguments which he had before joined with his pretended
friends in deriding.   He begged him to forgive his having treated them with levity, and him with the greateft
difrefpect ; and entreated his family to confider his generous friend, not only as the preferver of his life, but as
the reftorer of his morals.   Hence the whole family entertained the higheft idea of Mr. Grandifon's exalted
virtue and friendfhip ; and to ftrengthen their good opinion, the noble youth fhewed them the letters his friend
had wrote, with the hopes of inforcing his temporary
convictions, and drawing him from the fhameful purfuits
in which he was unhappily engaged.

The whole family were infpired with the utmoft gratitude.   The father was uneafy from his not knowing how
to acknowledge, according to the largenefs of his heart,
to a man of genteel circumftances, the obligations under
which he had laid them.   The mother, with an amiable
freedom, which the Italian ladies are unaccuftomed to exprefs, defired her Clementina to confider, as her fourth
brother, the preferver of the third ; and the Baron obferved, that he fhould never reft till his dear son
was rewarded in the manner he deferved.

C H A P. IV.

The Manner in which Mr. Grandifon *lived with this noble Family at* Bologna. *The Count of* Belvedere *falls in love with* Clementina, *whom Mr.* Grandifon *admires, yet is defired to talk to her in that Nobleman's Favour. That Lady is fufpected to be in love with Mr.* Grandifon, *who leaves* Italy. *Her ftrange Behaviour during his Abfence and her love for Mr.* Grandifon.

THE Barone was no fooner removed to Bologna than the whole family appeared ftudious to get Mr. Grandifon among them. The general made him promife, when his relations, as he termed them, at Bologna, could part with him, to favour them with his company at Naples. The bifhop, who fpent all the time he could fpare from his diocefe at Bologna, in compliment to Mr. Grandifon, his fourth brother, would have him give him leffons on the Englifh language. Our Milton's reputation had reached them, and the friendfhip that had fubfifted between him and a learned Italian nobleman, endeared his memory to them : he was therefore their principal author. As thefe lectures were ufually held in the wounded brother's chamber, in order to amufe him, he likewife became his fcholar. The father and the were frequently prefent, and the lovely Clementina feldom abfent : fhe alfo termed him her tutor ; and though fhe was feldomer prefent at thefe pleafing lectures than her brothers, fhe made a much greater proficiency than any of them.

In such company Mr. Grandison could not fail of passing his time very agreeably ; he was particularly honoured with the confidence of the Marchionefs, who opened her heart to him on every material occurrence that presented itself. Her lord, who is distinguished by his politenefs, was never better pleased than when he found them together ; and frequently, though they were not engaged in lectures, the lovely Clementina claimed a right to be present with her mother.

Things were in this fiuation when the young count of Belvedere, who had received his education in Spain, returned to Parma, and paying a visit to this noble family, saw and loved Clementina.   As the count was not only a man of sense, but had a handsome person, and a great fortune, they all thought that his alliance was very desirable.   The Marquis highly approved of it, and the Marchionefs had several conversations with Mr. Grandison on this subject : she thought it neceffary to know his thoughts on the occasion, as the Barone, unknown to him, had frequently declared, that he thought th▮ was no other way of rewarding his merit than by ▮ving him a relation to the family.   In the mean time Mr. Grandison, thus distinguished by all the persons of this noble house, and a daily witnefs of the innumerable excellencies of the lovely Clementina, found it impoffible not to suffer his vanity to be sometimes awakened, and ▮▮▮e his wishes of obtaining such a prize ; but he endeavoured to check the pleasing idea the moment he found it play about his heart, for he would have thought any attempt to recommend himself to the young lady's favour, though only by his looks and affiduities, a breach of that generous truft and confidence which they all repo-fed in him.

Mean while the rebellion breaking out in Scotland, Mr. Grandifon being known to be warm in the intereft of his country, was often obliged to enter into debates, which he fincerely wifhed to avoid. It was not doubted that the fuccefs of the rebels would be attended with the reftoration of the Romifh religion ; and Clementina was in particular pleafed with the thought, that her heretick tutor would then take refuge in the bofom of the mother church : fhe even took great delight in faying things of this nature in the language he taught her, and which fhe now fpoke very intelligibly.

Mr. Grandifon now formed the refolution of retiring from Italy, and vifiting fome of the German courts. This he communicated to the Marchionefs, who ex-preffed her concern at the thoughts of his leaving them, and prevailed on him to defer his departure for fome time ; but hinted her and her lord's apprehenfions of his being in love with Clementina. He convinced her that he had behaved with the utmoft honour in this particu-lar, fhe fo fully fatisfied the Marquis, that, on their daughter's abfolutely refufing the Count of Belvedere, they defired him to talk to her in favour of that no-bleman. The young lady and Mr. Grandifon had a conference on this fubject, while the Marquis and the Marchionefs, unknown to either of them, had placed themfelves to liften to their difcourfe in a clofet adjoin-ing to the room, and which communicated to another room, as well as to that they were in : however, they had not the leaft reafon to be difpleafed with their con-verfation.

The time of Mr. Grandifon's departure now drawing near, and the young lady repeatedly refufing the Count of

Belvedere, the Barone, unknown to his friend, declared
in his favour. His relations objected difficulties with re-
spect to his religion and his country, on which he desired they would permit his talking to him on those sub-
jects, and difcourfing with his fifter on her motives for refufing the Count of Belvedere ; but this they would not
allow. The Marchionefs herfelf undertook to talk to
her daughter, and to demand of her, her reafons for dif-
liking all the propofals that had been made her ; but on
her clofeting the lovely Clementina, nothing was to be got
from her but tears : a filence, that had not the leaft appearance of fullennefs, had, for fome days, fhewn that a
deep melancholy had begun to take poffeffion of her
mind, and yet fhe appeared extremely offended at their at-
tributing it to love : however, her mother informed Mr.
Grandifon, that fhe could not help fufpecting, that unknown to herfelf, fhe was under the dominion of that paffion, from her never appearing chearful, but when taking
leffons for learning a language that was never like to be
of the leaft fervice to her. Her melancholy ftill encreaf-
ing, he was defired to talk with her. He did fo, and it
was obferved that fhe generally affumed a cheerful air
while he was prefent, and, though fhe faid little, appeared pleafed with every thing he faid to her ; but the moment
he left her, fhe ftudied to find opportunities of being alone.
Her parents, who were in the deepeft affliction, confult-
ed phyficians, who all declared that fhe was in love : fhe
was taxed with it, and the utmoft indulgence promifed her
with refpect to the object of her affection that fhe could
wifh ; but ftill fhe could not bear the imputation with
patience.

On the evening before the day appointed for Mr.

Grandifon's departure, this noble family made a fplendid entertainment in honour of a gueft who had laid them under fuch extraordinary obligations ; for they had the more readily brought themfelves to approve of his leaving them, from their defire to know how it would affect Clementina. That lady appeared at table, and, during the whole evening, fupported her part of the converfation with extraordinary vivacity ; and yet there appeared nothing in her looks or behaviour that feemed the leaft affected. When they thanked him for the pleafure he had given the whole family, fhe joined her acknowledgements ; and when they expreffed their wifhes to fee him again before he returned to England, fhe did the fame. Mr. Grandifon's heart was dilated, and he was overjoyed at feeing fuch a happy alteration. When he took leave of them, fhe ftood forward to receive his compliments. He offered to prefs her hand with his lips, but prefenting her cheek to him, My brother's deliverer, faid fhe, muft not affect this diftance, adding, God preferve my tutor wherever he goes ! May you never want fuch an agreeable friend as you have been to us ! And, in Englifh, God convert you, Chevalier !

As the Barone was not able to be with them, his friend went to take his leave of him, when, throwing his arms about him, he cried, O my Grandifon ! will you go ? Bleffings attend you ! but what will become of a brother and fifter, when they have loft you ? She muft, fhe fhall be yours—why will you leave us ? Mr. Grandifon was furprifed ! for he had never before been fo particular, and anfwered, It could not be, for there were a thoufand obftacles ;—All of which, returned the Barone, that depend on us, I don't doubt I fhall overcome. They then fettled a method of carrying on their correfpondence, and parted.

The next morning Mr. Grandifon fet out for In-fpruck, but on his arrival at that city, was deeply afflicted at receiving a letter by which he was informed that Clementina's chearful and lively behaviour had lafted no longer than the next day, and that her malady had returned with double force. She fhut herfelf up in her chamber without feeming to know that her woman was in it, or making any anfwer to the queftions fhe afked her ; but fetting her chair with its back towards her over againft a clofet, after a deep filence, leaned forwards, and in a low voice, feemed talking to a perfon in the clofet, crying, You fay he is actually gone ? Gone for ever ? No, not forever ! Who, Madam ? faid the woman.   To whom, pray, do you direct your difcourfe ?——We are all doubtlefs obliged to him, refumed fhe ; fo bravely to refcue my brother, and to purfue the bravoes, and, as my brother fays, to put him into his own chaife, and walk on foot by its fide.—Why, as you fay, the affaffins might have murdered him, or the horfes might have trampled him under their feet. Her woman then ftepped into the clofet, and in order to turn the courfe of her ideas, opened the door, and left it open, to try if that would divert her attention from the place ; but fhe ftill talked calmly, as if to fomebody in it, then burfting into a faint laugh, fhe cried, In love ! that is fuch a filly whim ; and yet I love every body better than myfelf. At this inftant the Marchionefs entering the room, Clementina rofe in hafte, and fhutting the clofet door, as if fomebody had been hid there, threw herfelf at her feet, crying, my dear Mamma, forgive me for all the trouble I have caufed you—But I will, I muft be God's child as well as your's, I will retire into a convent.

Every thing that medicine could do was now tried : but her confessor, though an honest and worthy man, had filled her mind with fears and terrors. He observed the favour Mr. Grandison was in with the whole family, and dreading left his influence might have such an effect as to withdraw this lady from the bosom of the church, had raised such a conflict in her heart, between her piety, which was ardent and sincere, and her gratitude and sensibility, as her tender frame was unable to bear.

In the city of Florence is a family of distinguished rank and honour, the ladies of which have a friend who lives with them named Beaumont, who in the early part of life was defrauded of her fortune by an uncle. She is an English protestant, and is greatly esteemed for her genius, and the goodness of her heart. These ladies, with this their companion, were one day visiting at the Marchese della Porretta's, when the distressed mother told them the mournful tale ; and they thinking nothing that could be effected by human prudence impossible to Mrs. Beaumont, desired, that the young lady might be entrusted to her care at their house in Florence. To this they immediately agreed, and they took her with them. Mrs. Beaumont soon engaged the unhappy Clementina's affections, and, by her very artful management, found means to prevail on her to reveal the cause of her melancholy, and that it arose from her regard of Mr. Grandison. Her hopes that this absence would restore her tranquillity, had made her behave with such steadiness at his departure ; but she was not long able to maintain so great a part ; yet she still professed that she would never marry one who by his religion was an enemy to the faith, in which she had never wavered, and which, she observed, she would never change, were an earthly crown to be placed on the head of the man she loved, to be the reward.

Upon this, Mrs. Beaumont wrote an affecting letter to the Marchionefs, in which she gave her a particular account of this converfation ; and that lady, in return, fent her an anfwer, filled with the warmeft expreffions of gratitude, inclofing it in a letter to her daughter, wherein she endeavoured to give her all the confolation poffible, inviting her and her amiable friend to Bologna, and promifing, in the name of her father and brothers, a moft indulgent welcome, with the gratification of all her wifhes. The lady Clementina became much eafier and more compofed, on receiving thefe affurances, and returned to Bologna, with a more ferene and fettled mind than she enjoyed at her leaving that city.

CHAP. V.

The whole family being informed of Clementina's *Paffion, fent for Mr.* Grandifon. *His Reception at his Return. They propofe his marrying the Lady ; but though he loves her with the greateft Tendernefs, the Conditions are fuch as he cannot comply with, on which he again leaves* Italy.

THE whole family were defired to affemble upon this occafion, when, by common confent, it was agreed that Mr. Grandifon fhould be fent for. That gentleman was then at Vienna, and Jeronymo, in his letter, congratulated him on his having it now in his power to reward him ; hinting in general, that the conditions

would be fuch as he could not fail of thinking highly to
his advantage.   This news greatly affected Mr. Grand-
ſon ; for, from his knowledge of the lady and the whole
family, he was afraid the articles of reſidence and religion would not be eaſily compromiſed ; on which account
he ſummoned up all his prudence to keep alive his fears,
and ſuſpend every flattering hope.

He inſtantly returned to Bologna, where, on his arrival, he was received with all the marks of friendſhip and
eſteem by the Marquis and the Biſhop.   The Barone,
who ſtill kept his chamber, embracing him, ſaid, Now
is the affair I have ſo long had in view, determined.   O
Chevalier, you'll be a happy man ; Clementina will be
your's, and you will be Clementina's.   Now do I indeed
embrace my brother—But I won't detain you ; haſte to
the happy girl, who is with her mother, and both are
ready to welcome you.   Mr. Grandiſon was then conducted into the Marchioneſs's drawing-room, where he
found that lady richly dreſſed, with the lovely Clementina alſo elegantly dreſſed, and ſtanding by her chair ;
while her natural modeſty, heightened by a glowing con-
ſcioufneſs that ſeemed to ariſe from the occaſion, gave her
advantages fuperior to her richeſt jewels.   The Marchioneſs behaved to him with great tenderneſs and reſpect,
apologized for her daughter's ſilence and confuſion ; and,
on her retiring, congratulated him on the happineſs intended him, obſerving that ſhe would leave particular
ſubjects to be diſcourſed of between the Biſhop and him,
adding, that the ſame thing ſhould be done for Clementina, as if ſhe had married the man they wiſhed her to
have, when they imagined her affections entirely diſen-
gaged.   Mr. Grandiſon applauded her goodneſs, and ſhe
added, that ſhe did not doubt his loving Clementina

more than any other lady. He returned, that he had
never seen one he could have loved with such tenderness,
had he not put a restraint upon himself, from the high
notions they entertained of their rank and quality, from
the difference of religion, and from the confidence the
family reposed in him ; he therefore assured the Mar-
chioness, that not having presumed to encourage hopes of
the happiness that now seemed to await him, he could
hardly yet flatter himself that he should enjoy such felicity. She answered, that he deserved it all : he knew the
value they had for him : Clementina's regard was found-
ed on virtue, and she did not doubt but all that depended
on him would, as well from generosity as gratitude, be
complied with. The Marquis, who entered soon after,
behaved with the same indulgence, letting him know
that his son the Bishop would discourse with him upon
terms. A great fortune, besides a noble estate bequeath-
ed her by her two grandfathers, was proposed, and his
father was to be invited over to grace their nuptials.

The Bishop at last made the dreaded proposals, with
which neither his conscience nor his love for his country
would suffer him to comply. He was to make a formal
renunciation of his religion, and to settle in Italy, and
only be allowed once in two or three years to go to England, if he pleased, for two or three months : and if
their daughter should desire it, she might once in her life
be carried thither on a visit of curiosity, and stay there
the time they should limit. The Bishop, who was amazed at his scruples, in vain endeavoured to convince him
of what he called his errors ; for he could not change his
religion without conviction : he even reproached him
with obstinacy, ingratitude, and cruelty. The General,

D

who was now at Bologna, raved, threatened, and treated him with contempt, while the Marquis began to confider him as unworthy of the honour defigned him. In what diftrefs was Mr. Grandifon involved, in being thus obliged to deny himfelf the deareft wifh of his heart, and to difappoint the warm expectations of thofe who had a fincere value for him ! But when his dear Jeronymo intreated his compliance ; when the tender mother entreated him to have pity on her heart, and her poor child's head ; and when the gentle, the lovely Clementina, urged him for his foul's fake, to embrace the doctrines of her holy mother the church : how was his mind torn by the contending paffions which tortured his breaft ! But he was fully fatisfied with his own faith, and had infuperable objections to that which they defired him to embrace ; and if he complied, his confcience and his country were to be the facrifice. Yet he ftudied for a compromife. Clementina was very dear to him, and he then beheld graces in her which he had hitherto ftruggled to behold with indifference. He propofed to live one year in Italy, and one in England, by turns, if their dear Clementina would confent to live with him there ; if not, he propofed to pafs only three months in every year in his native country. He offered to leave her entirely at her liberty in the article of religion ; and, in cafe of children by the marriage, the daughters to be educated by her, and the fons by him ; a condition to which the Pope himfelf, it was prefumed, would not refufe his fanction. To this the unhappy Clementina would have confented, and earneftly endeavoured to procure the confent of her friends. But no arguments could prevail on them to allow their daughter to marry a proteftant. This determination was followed by the moft diftrefsful fcenes : the mother, indeed, feemed in a manner neutral ; and the Barone remained ftill firm in Mr. Grandifon's intereft ; but the Marquis, the General, the Bifhop, and the whole Urbino branch of the family, were immoveable. The General treated him even with an infolent arrogance, and imagining that Mr. Grandifon had ufed fome art to engage his fifter's affections, pretended to have a right to call him to account for it : but notwithftanding Mr. Grandifon's being deeply diftreffed, he anfwered the General's paffionate fpeeches with fpirit ; but let him know that nothing fhould make him attempt the life of the brother of his friend. The rigour of their behaviour was now extended even to the unhappy Clementina, and Mr. Grandifon in vain recommended their treating her with indulgence. He was defired to depart from Bologna, and Clementina was not permitted to fee him, though fhe begged on her knees to have a parting interview. At hearing of his being gone, her grief moved every one to pity, and this fubfided into fits, the deepeft melancholy, and filence.

CHAP. VI.

Mr. Grandifon *faves Mr.* Danby's *Life. The manner
in which Sir* Thomas Grandifon *lived while his Son
was on his Travels. His Death, and the Treatment
Mrs.* Oldham *received from Sir* Charles's *Sifters.*

MR. Grandifon no fooner left Italy than he proceeded to Paris, to wait there for orders from his father to return to his native country. While he was in
France, he paid a vifit to Mr. Danby, an eminent merchant of great integrity, to whom his father remitted
money for his ufe. With this gentleman he had been
before acquainted, and having now fpent two days with
him in the city, he accompanied him to a little lone
houfe in the Cambrefis, which that gentleman ufed to
term his dormitory. Mr. Grandifon had only one fervant with him, who lay in a little room over the ftable,
with a man-fervant of Mr. Danby's, there being conve-
niences in the houfe only for Mr. Danby, a friend, and
two women-fervants. About midnight Mr. Grandifon
was alarmed by hearing a noife at the window of Mr.
Danby's room, when inftantly flipping on his cloathes,
and drawing his fword, he ran thither juft as a villain
with a large knife in his hand had feized Mr. Danby's
throat, who till then was found afleep. The fkin of his
neck, and one of his hands, which he had lifted up to de-
fend himfelf, were flightly wounded, when Mr. Grandifon run the ruffian into the fhoulder with his fword, and
at the fame moment threw him with violence from the

bed againſt the door ; on which he roared out, that he was a dead man. By that time a ſecond fellow, who had got to the window, was half in, when calling to a third below to haſte up after him, Mr. Grandiſon ran to the ſecond fellow, who then fired a piſtol, but happily miſſed him ; and feeling the point of the ſword in his arm, threw himſelf, with a little of Mr. Grandiſon's help, upon the third ruffian, who was mounting the ladder, and knocked him off; after which both made their eſcape. Mean while the aſſaſſin within had fainted away, and the two maids let in Mr. Grandiſon's and Mr. Danby's ſervants, who had been alarmed by the ſcreams of the women from their window, and the report of the piſtol. The two footmen having, by Mr. Grandiſon's order, bound up the ruffian's ſhoulder, and carried him into the hall, he came to himſelf, and offered to make a full confeſſion ; and being carried before a magiſtrate, laid open the whole villainy.

Mr. Danby had a brother of very abandoned pinciples, to whom he had frequently given large ſums, which he had ſquandered away in his debaucheries. He had alſo ſettled a thouſand guineas on each of the children of his brother, who had the folly and impudence to make a demand of the ſame ſum, pleading that he had as much right to it as they ; and enraged at his meeting with a refuſal, formed a deſign to get the poſſeſſion of his whole fortune : for Mr. Danby being a batchelor, and known to have an averſion to the thoughts of making his will, this wretch had hired theſe ruffians to murder him ; and that the fact might have the appearance of being done by robbers, the houſe was to have been plundered, as ſoon as the horrid fact was perpetrated. The villains were each to receive a thoufand crowns on this unnatural monfter's getting poffeffion of his brother's fortune ; and they had fifty crowns a piece paid them in hand. Their bafe employer waited the event at Calais ; and being foon informed of what had happened, paffed over to Dover. The two men who had efcaped, were difabled by their bruifes from flying far, and were apprehended ; but the wounded man having loft much blood, did not recover : the furvivors were ordered for execution ; but Mr. Danby interceding for them, they were fent to the gallies.

During the time that Mr. Grandifon was facrificing the deareft wifhes of his heart to his religion, and his love of his country, and was expofed to dangers that called forth all his courage, his father was indulging his love of pleafure. He placed over his daughters, as governefs, the widow of one of his companions, named Oldham, whofe fortune had not held out as Sir Thomas's had done. This lady had fine qualities, was well defcended, handfome, and an œconomift ; but fhe foon became fo unhappily fenfible of Sir Thomas's favours and prefents, that in a little more than a twelve month, fhe was obliged to come up to town, where fhe lay in. The eldeft of thefe young ladies, being at that time about nineteen, and the youngeft fixteen years old, they had fuch fpirit as to oppofe this lady's return to her office ; and undertook to manage every thing themfelves at their capital feat in Hampfhire. But Sir Thomas having another feat in Effex, carried Mrs. Oldham thither ; and for fome time every body apprehended that they were married. Sir Thomas was highly difpleafed at his daughters for oppofing the return of their governefs ; and he had another miftrefs in town, who had a tafte for all its gaieties.

The young ladies were now treated with great feverity by Sir Thomas, and his fon had not been long abroad, when they were forbid to correfpond with him, left his follies fhould be the fubject of their correfpondence ; and he alfo ordered their brother not to write to them. This prohibition gave thefe ladies the moft fenfible concern, as they dreaded its laying a foundation for their being treated with indifference by their brother, on whom, as their mother had foretold, they were likely, if he furvived their father, to have too great a dependence. But though Sir Thomas fhewed not the leaft tendernefs for his daughters, he, in all companies, gloried in his fon, who, he obferved, was all that was dutiful, brave, worthy, and pious ; alleging to his intimate friends, that the reafon of his permitting his being fo long abfent, was, that his fon's morals and his own were fo different, that he fhould be afhamed of his fuperiority ; but that he intended to alter his courfe of life, and then he would fend for him. In the mean while Mrs. Farnborough, the woman he lived with when in town, being feized with the fmall pox, died ; on which, Sir Thomas was fo much affected, that he left the town, and in purfuance of his temporary good refolutions, lived with his daughters, and talked of fending for his fon ; and for fome months behaved like a man of fenfe and underftanding.

About the time of Mrs. Farnborough's being taken ill, Lord L——returning from his travels, brought Sir Thomas fome prefents from his fon, who took all opportunities to fend him curiofities, fome of which were of confiderable value, and ferved to fhew both his duty and œconomy. Sir Thomas appeared fond of Lord —— ; and on his retiring to Grandifon Hall, after Mrs. Farnborough's

death, gave him an invitation to vifit him there. Hence
that nobleman attended him at the Hall, where he fell in
love with the eldeft of the young ladies, to whom he re-
vealed his paffion.   She referred herfelf wholly to her father ; but though this match would have been highly to
her advantage, Sir Thomas abfolutely refufed his confent.

At length, Sir Thomas refolved to regulate his affairs,
preparative to the leave he intended to give his fon to return home ; but he knew not what to do with Mrs. Oldham and two children he had by her. He made no doubt
of his fon's having heard of his guilty commerce with her ;
but did not chufe that he fhould find her living with him
as a miftrefs in one of the family feats.   He was alfo unwilling to ufe her unhandfomely, and thought himfelf
obliged to provide for the children he had by her.

While he was thus contriving how to make the beft
appearance before his fon, whofe charaƈter for virtue and
prudence made him half afraid of him, he received a propofal of marriage for the young gentleman from one of
the firft men in the kingdom, whofe daughter, accompanying her brother and his lady in a tour to France and
Italy, fell in love with Mr. Grandifon at Florence.   Sir
Thomas had feveral meetings on this fubjeƈt, both with
the brother and the Earl his father ; and was fo fond of
bringing it to bear, that he had thoughts of referving to
himfelf an annuity, and, in favour of this match, making over the whole eftate to his fon ; and aƈtually
fent him this propofal.   But Mr. Grandifon, in his anfwer, obferved, that, if this arofe from his generofity, af-
feƈtion, and indulgence he had fo often experienced, he
could not bear it ; but if it proceeded from propofals

made to him, God forbid, faid he, that I fhould give
your name to a woman, however illuftrious in her defcent
and however wealthy, whofe friends could offer fuch conditions to my father.　On thff anfwer, Sir Thomas refolved to fufpend the treaty of marriage till his fon's arrival.

While Sir Thomas was planning future fchemes of
life, and had actually begun to treat with Mrs. Oldham,
who defiring to reform her conduct, agreed to retire at
the firft word ; he was feized with a violent fever, which
in three days deprived him of the ufe of his reafon.　He
was at this time with Mrs. Oldham at his feat in Effex ;
and the phyficians foon giving her no hopes of his recovery, fhe wrote to acquaint the two young ladies with his
danger, who, a few days after, difpatched a letter to their
brother, who was waiting at Paris, expecting to receive
permiffion from his father to return home.　On the elev-
enth day of his illnefs, Sir Thomas coming a little to
himfelf, knew his daughters, and wept over them.　He
then wifhed he had been kinder to them.　He was fenfible of his danger, and feveral times lifted up his feeble
hands and dying eyes, repeating, God is juft.　I have
been very wicked !——Repentance ! repentance ! how
hard a tafk ! And Mrs. Oldham entering the room, Oh
Mrs. Oldham, what is the world now ? What would I
give ? But repent ! repent ! repent ! Put your good refolutions in practice, left I have more fouls to anfwer
for than my own.　Soon after his delirium returned, and
he expired.

Now the two daughters, their coufin Grandifon, and
Mrs. Oldham for her own fecurity, put their refpective
feals on every place at that houfe, where any thing valu-

able was suppofed to be depofited ; and Mr. Grandifon
affuming the management, turned out Mrs. Oldham,
permitting her to take with her only one fuit of cloaths
befides thofe fhe had on. She wept bitterly, complaining of harfh treatment, but met with no pity, and was
referred by Mr. Grandifon for more rigorous juftice to
his abfent coufin. She appealed to the ladies, but they
reproached her with having lived a life of fhame, obferving
that her punifhment was but beginning, that their brother
would do her juftice : he was a man of virtue, and they
were fure would look upon her with abhorrence. Thus
this unhappy woman already received a fevere inftance of
the change of her fortune, and had two much reafon to
believe that they would eafily incenfe their brother againft
her, as his fortune had been leffened by his father's pro-
fufion. The few relations fhe had living were people of
honour, who, fince her living with Sir Thomas, had re-
nounced all correfpondence with her ; and fhe had one
fon by her hufband, befides the two by Sir Thomas, to
provide for.

C H A P. VII.

Sir Charles *returns to* England. *His engaging Behaviour
to his Sifters, and to Mrs.* Oldham.

THE affairs of the family were in this fituation
when Sir Charles arrived. He returned no anfwer
to his fifters' letter, but inftantly fet out for Calais, embarked, and the fame day in which he landed arrived at
his late father's houfe in St. James's fquare. How awful

to the fifters, after an abfence of eight or nine years, muft be the firft appearance of a brother on whom their fortunes entirely depended, and to whom they had been accufed by their father, now fo lately departed, of want of duty ! He alighted from his poft-chaife at the door, and his two fifters met him in the hall. They remembered the graceful youth of feventeen who had left them, with his fine curling auburn locks waving on his fhoulders, intelligence fparkling in his fine eyes, and his lively features fweetened by good humour ; and, forgetting the womanly beauties into which their own features were ripened, feemed not to expect that manly ftature and air, and that equal vivacity and intrepidity, with a noble countenance, that then appeared more than ufually folemn, from his having in his thoughts an unburied and beloved father. O my brother ! faid Caroline, meeting him with open arms, but fhrinking from his embrace, may I fay my brother ? and was juft fainting. He clafped her, and fupported her in his arms. Charlotte, the youngeft, affected at his prefence, and furprifed at her fifter's emotion, ran back into the room they had left, and threw herfelf upon a fettee. Her brother followed her, foothing Mifs Caroline, with his arm round her waift, and with eyes of expectation, cried, My Charlotte ! holding out his inviting hand, and hafting towards the fettee. She then found her feet, and throwing her arms about his neck, he folded both of his fifters to his bofom, crying, Receive, my deareft fifters, receive your brother, your friend. Affure yourfelves of my unabated love. That affurance, they cried, was balm to their hearts ; and when each was feated, he fitting over againft them, looked firft on one, then on the other ; and taking

E

each by the hand, Charming women ! faid he, how I admire my fifters ! I don't doubt that you have minds anfwerable to your perfons. What pleafure, what pride fhall I take in my fifters ! My dear Charlotte ! faid Mifs Caroline, taking her fifter's other hand, has not our brother all the brother in his face ? His goodnefs only looks ftronger and more perfect. What was I afraid of ? My heart alfo funk, I knew not why, faid Charlotte : but we feared—— indeed, Sir, we both feared——O my brother ! tears trickling down the cheeks of each——we did not mean to be undutiful——Love your brother, my dear fifters, he returned, as he will endeavour to deferve your love. My mother's daughters could not be undutiful——miftake only !—unhappy mifapprehenfion ! He then preffed the hands of each with his lips, arofe, went to the window, and wiped his eyes :—then turning towards them, added, Permit me, my dear fifters, to retire for a moment ; my father demands this tribute. They waited on him to his apartment with filent refpect. No ceremony I hope, my Caroline, my Charlotte, he refumed ; we were true fifters and brother a few years ago : fee your Charles as you faw him then } and don't let abfence, which has en-creafed my love, leffen yours. Each fifter then took a hand, and would have kiffed it ; but he clafped his arms about them both, and faluted them. He caft his eyes on his father's and mother's pictures with fome emotion, then on them, and again faluting each of them, they withdrew with tears of joy trickling down their cheeks.

Sir Charles in half an hour rejoined them in another drefs, and again faluted them with an air of tendernefs that banifhed fear, and left room for nothing but love. Soon after their coufin Grandifon came in ; and after the firft compliments, the ladies retiring, that gentleman touched upon the circumftances of Sir Thomas's illnefs and death ; inveighing againft Mrs. Oldham, telling Sir Charles what they had done, and exclaiming againft her for the ftate fhe had lived in, and her unwillingnefs to refign the care of Sir Thomas, in his illnefs, to his daughters ; and particularly for having the affurance to put her feal with theirs to the cabinets and clofets that were fuppofed to contain what was valuable. He then afked Sir Charles, if he was not pleafed with what they had done as to that vile woman ? But he only obferved, that he believed every thing was defigned for the beft. Mr. Grandifon then ridiculed her grief and mortification at being obliged to leave the houfe, where fhe had fo long reigned Lady Paramount. Sir Charles afked if they had found a will ? and was anfwered, that they looked in every probable place, but found none. I intend, faid Sir Charles, to inter the venerable remains with thofe of my mother, which I know was his defire. An elegant, but not fumptuous monument, fhall be erected to the memory of both, with a modeft infcription, that fhall be rather a matter of inftruction to the living, than a panegyrick on the deceafed. The funeral fhall be decent, not oftentatious ; and the difference of the expence fhall be privately applied to affift diftreffed houfekeepers, or fome of my father's poor tenants who have large families, and have endeavoured by their induftry to maintain them. And this was foon after carried in execution.

The folemnity was no fooner over, than Sir Charles, leaving every thing as he found it at Grandifon Hall, came to town, and, in the prefence of his fifters, broke the feals they had affixed to the cabinets and efcrutores in

the houfe there; and having made memorandums of the
contents of many papers, went with his fifters to the
houfe in Effex, and when there, told them it was neceffary for Mrs. Oldham, who had lodgings at a farm-haufe
in the neighbourhood, to be prefent at breaking the feals,
as fhe had affixed hers; and accordingly fent for her. She
came with fear and trembling, when Sir Charles, not expecting her fo foon, was in his ftable, with the groom
and coachman, looking at his horfes, which were fome of
the fineft hunters and racers in England. She was fhewn,
by miftake, into the room where the two ladies were, and
at feeing them was in great confufion, wept, courtefied,
and, on Mifs Caroline's blaming her maid for bringing
her to them, begged pardon, and was withdrawing, but
ftopped on that lady's faying, My brother, not we, fent
for you, I affure you, Madam. He fays it is neceffary,
as you thought fit to put your feal with ours, that you
fhould be prefent at the breaking them. Prepare yourfelf
to fee him : you feem mighty unfit——No wonder ! Indeed I am unfit, very unfit, faid the poor woman : let
me, ladies, befpeak your generofity ; a little of your pity ;
a little of your countenance ; I am indeed an unhappy
woman ! And fo you deferve to be, faid Mifs Caroline.
I am fure we are the fufferers. And fo you have put
yourfelf into mourning, Madam ! Pretty doings ; Indeed, ladies, faid Mrs. Oldham, I am a real mourner.
Here, ladies, are the keys of the ftores, of the confec-
tionary, and of the wine vault. I thought it beft to keep
them till I could deliver them to your or Sir Charles's
order. I have not, ladies, been a bad manager, confidered as a houfe-keeper ; all I have in the world is under
the feals. I am at yours and your brother's mercy.

You'll foon know, Madam, faid Mifs Charlotte, what you have to truft to from him.

Sir Charles entered, and faw her ftanding pale and trembling near the door. He bowed to her. Mrs. Oldham, I prefume, faid he—Pray, Madam, be feated ; I fent to you that you might fee the feals broken—Pray, Madam, fit down,. added he, taking her hand, and leading her to a chair not far diftant from his fifters ; and then fitting in one between them and her, Pray, Madam, compofe yourfelf, added he, with pity in his eyes ; and then turned to his fifters, to allow her time to recover herfelf. She was relieved by a flood of tears, and tried to fupprefs her audible fobs, which he would not feem to hear. Her emotions then attracting the eyes of his fifters, he took them off by afking them fomething about a picture that hung on the other fide of the room. Then drawing his chair nearer to the unhappy woman, and again taking her trembling hand, faid, I am not a ftranger, Mrs. Oldham, to your melancholy ftory. Don't be difcompofed. See in me a friend ready to thank you for all your paft good offices, and to forget all miftaken ones. This was more than fhe could bear ; fhe threw herfelf at his feet, when raifing her to her chair, he added, Poor Mrs. Oldham was unhappily carelefs, yet I have been told he loved you, and that you merited his love. Your misfortunes threw you into the knowledge of our family. You have been a faithful manager of the affairs of this houfe. By written evidences I can juftify you ; evidences that I am fure none here will difpute. Mr. Grandifon, who is a good-natured man, but a little hafty, has told me, that he treated you with unkindnefs. He thought you wrong for infifting to put your feal ; but he

was miftaken, you did right. O brother ! O brother !
faid both the ladies at once, half in admiration, though
half vexed. Bear with me, my fifters, faid he ; we have
all fomething to be forgiven for. They knew not but
they might be concerned in the admonition from what
their father had written of them. He then mentioned
chocolate being brought in, and being defirous, of reliev-
ing Mrs. Oldham by fome little employment, defired her
to be fo obliging as to fee it made.

She had no fooner left the room, than, addreffing himfelf to the ladies, My dear fifters, faid he, let me, on
this occafion, defire you to think favourably of me. I
don't confider this poor woman on the foot of her own
merits with refpect to us : the memory of our father is
concerned : fhe is intitled to juftice, for its own fake ;
to generofity, for ours ; to kindnefs, for my father's. In
feveral of his letters to me, he praifes Mrs. Oldham's
œconomy, and he had a right to do what he would with
his own fortune. It was not ours till now. Whatever
he has left us he might have leffened. The œconomy is
all that concerns us in the point of intereft, and that is
in her favour. He might have given Mrs. Oldham a
title to a name that would have commanded our refpect,
if not our reverence. You have enlarged minds ; and
are the daughters of the moft charitable, the moft for-
giving of women ; and I was willing to judge of her behaviour, before I recommended her to your humanity.
Is fhe not humbled enough ? From my foul, I pity her.
She loved my father, I don't doubt mourns for him in
fecret, yet does not dare to plead her love. I would now
confider her only as one who has executed a principal office in this houfe ; and it will become us to behave to her

in fuch a manner as to make the woild think we confider her only in that light.

When they had drank chocolate, he told Mrs. Oldham, he was ready to attend her, and defired his fifters
to give them their company. On their coming to the
chamber in which Sir Thomas died, Mrs. Oldham turned pale,and begged to wait in the adjoining drawing room.
Poor woman, cried he, how unhappily is fhe circum-
ftanced ! She dares not, before us, fhew the tendernefs
which is the glory of her fex, and of human nature ! On
opening one of the cabinets in that chamber, they found
a beautiful little cafket with a paper wafered upon it, on
which was written, *My wife's jewels.* Sir Charles afked his fifters, if they had not received their mother's jewels, and they anfwering, that their father had faid they
fhould be theirs on their marriage, he immediately prefented them this cafket, which they retired to open, while
their brother was taking minutes of papers. Befides the
jewels, they found in it three purfes, in two of which
were a confiderable number of old broad pieces, with
fome bank-notes and India-bonds. The third parcel
was thus labelled, *For my beloved fon : in acknowledge-
ment of his duty to his father and me, from infancy to this
hour ; of his love to his fifters ; of the generofity of his
temper ; of his love of truth, and of his modefty, courage,
benevolence, fteadinefs of mind, docility, and other great
and amiable qualities, by which he gives a moral affurance
of his making a good man. God grant it ! Amen.*

This purfe the ladies immediately carried to their
brother, when having read the label, Excellent woman,
faid he, being dead fhe yet fpeaks ; may her pious prayer
be anfwered ! Then opening the purfe, he found five cor-

onation medals of different princes, a gold fnuff-box, in which were three diamond rings, and a miniature picture of his mother, an admirable likenefs, fet in gold. Neglecting the reft, he took it out, gazed at it in filence, kiffed it, and put it next his heart. The ladies then told him what was in the other purfes, and offered him the bonds, notes, and money ; when afking if there were no directions upon either, they anfwered, No. He then obferving there might be a difference in their value, emptied them upon the table, and mixing the contents of both together, added, Thus mingled, you, my fifters, will equally divide them between you. This picture, placing his hand on his bofom, where it ftill was, is of infinitely more value than what all the three purfes contain befides.

Sir Charles and his fifters having examined every other place in this apartment, he followed Mrs. Oldham to her's ; where, fhewing him the clofet in which was contained all fhe was worth, fhe complained of Mr. Grandifon's refufing to let her take out of it 50l. He told her fhe might affure herfelf of juftice, and breaking the feal, defired her to produce what fhe thought proper for him to take account of. He was obliged to check the curiofity of his fifters, who would fain have examined her drawers. She fhewed him the cabinet in which was contained all the money, notes, and fecurities fhe had honeftly faved. Mifs Caroline afked to what amount ? No matter, fifter, faid Sir Charles. You hear, Mrs. Oldham fays, they are honeftly faved. I dare fay my father's bounty enabled his meaneft fervants to fave money. I would not keep one that I thought did not. I make no comparifon. Mrs. Oldham, you are a gentlewoman. I believe, faid Mrs. Oldham, looking afraid of the cenfures of the ladies, there is near 1200l. They appeared furprifed at the largenefs of the fum, and obferved, that they fhould often have been glad of having as many fhillings between them. Sir Charles afked what occafion had they for more than current money? but added, that now they had a claim to independency, he hoped either of their ftores would exceed that fum. Mrs. Oldham, then trembling, faid, In this private drawer are fome prefents—I difclaim them : if you'll believe me, ladies, I never wifhed for them, offering to pull out the drawer. Forbear, Mrs. Oldham, faid Sir Charles, both the prefents and money are yours : never will I either difparage or diminifh my father's bounty. Ha had a right to do as he pleafed. Had he made a will, would they not have been yours ?—If you, my fifters, if you, Mrs. Oldham, can tell me any thing he but intended to do for any of his people, I will execute that intention with the fame exactnefs as if he had inferted it in a will. Shall we do nothing but legal juftice ?—The law was not made for a man of confcience.

When Sir Charles had examined and taken minutes of every thing in this houfe, he delivered to Mrs. Oldham the key of her apartment, ordering the houfe-keeper to affift her in the removal of her effects when fhe pleafed, and to allow her to come and go at all times with the fame freedom and civility as if fhe had never left the houfe. Then, addreffing himfelf to his fifters, he faid, You may confider the juftice I am willing to do to perfons who can claim only juftice from me, as an earneft that I will do more than juftice for you. You fhould have been the firft to have found the fruits of my love, had I not feared that prudence would have narrowed my intentions, I am forry, my dear fifters, for the fake of your fpirits, that

you are left in my power. The beft of women always
feared that it would be fo ; but as foon as I can, you
fhall be abfolutely independent on your brother. Both
Caroline and Charlotte expreffed their gratitude by their
tears, telling him that their being in the power of fuch a
brother was their higheft felicity.

Some time after, Sir Charles, at parting with Mrs.
Oldham, told her he fhould be glad to know how fhe difpofed of herfelf, every unhappy perfon having a right to
the good offices of thofe who are lefs embarraffed ; and
that when fhe was fettled, fhe would let him know the
ftate of her affairs, and what fhe propofed to do with thofe
intitled to her care, and fhe fhould find that her confidence
was not ill-placed. Mrs. Oldham, the firft opportunity,
prefented him a written eftimate of all fhe was worth,
and an account of the manner in which fhe propofed to
live ; on which he had the generofity to fettle an annuity
upon her for the fake of her fons by his father.

As Sir Charles found that his father had left his affairs
embarraffed, he difpofed of his hunters, racers, and dogs,
took a furvey of the timber upon his eftate, and felled
what would have been worfe for ftanding ; but for the
fake of pofterity, planted an oakling for every oak he cut
down. The fale of the timber he felled in Hampfhire,
lying convenient for water carriage for the ufe of the gov-
ernment, furnifhed him with a confiderable fum. He
then went to examine his eftate in Ireland, paid off a
mortgage upon it, and ordered great improvements.

Two or three months after Sir Charles's arrival in
England, Lord L. came to town from Scotland, and paid
him his firft vifit ; when his Lordfhip mentioning his love
for Mifs Caroline, and fhe acknowledging her regard for

him, he introduced him to her, and joining their hands, held them between both his, saying, With pleasure do I join hands, where such worthy hearts are united. From this time, my Lord, do me the honour to look upon me as your brother. My father was a little embarrassed in his affairs, and was perhaps loth they should early claim another protection ; but if he had lived to make himself easy, he would doubtless have made them happy. He has left that duty upon me, and I will perform it. Miss Caroline's joy rendered her unable to speak, and my Lord was extremely affected. Miss Charlotte was moved with this scene, and lifting up her hands and eyes, prayed, that God would make his power as large as his heart. And has not my Charlotte, said he, turning towards her, some happy man whom she can distinguish by her love ? You, my sisters, are equally dear to me. Come, Charlotte, make me your confidant, and your inclinations shall direct my choice.

Before the marriage Sir Charles gave his sister a paper sealed up. Receive this, my Caroline, said he, as from your father's bounty, in compliance with what your mother, had she lived, would have wished. When you oblige Lord L—— with one hand, make him this present with the other ; and thus intitle yourself to all the gratitude with which his worthy heart will overflow. I have only done my duty in performing an article of the will I have made in my own mind for my father. He then saluted her, and withdrew before she broke the seal ; and when she did, she found it contained bank notes for 10,000l. She threw herself into a chair, and for some time was unable to rise ; but recovering herself, she hurried out to find her brother, and was told he was in his fifter's apartment. She ran thither, and found Charlotte was in tears, Sir Charles having juft left her. What ails my Charlotte ? faid fhe. O Caroline, cried the other, this brother ! there is no bearing his generous goodnefs. See that deed ! She took it up, and finding it was for the fame fum he had given her, and to carry intereft, they congratulated and wept over each other, as if diftreffed. Caroline found out her brother, but when fhe approached him, could only exprefs her gratitude by lifting up her hands and eyes. He had no fooner raifed and feated her, than the equally grateful Charlotte entered, when placing her next her fifter, and drawing a chair for himfelf, he took the hand of each, and then faid, My dear fifters, you are too fenfible of thefe inftances of my brotherly love. It has pleafed God to deprive us of our father and mother, and we muft fupply their lofs to each other. Confider me as an executor of a will that ought to have been made, and perhaps would, had there been time. My circum-ftances are greater than I expected ; greater, I dare fay, than my father thought they would be ; and I could not do lefs than I have done. You don't know how much you'll oblige me if you never fay another word upon this fubject. Soon after this, Caroline was married to Lord L———, who carried her down with him to Scotland, where fhe was greatly admired and efteemed by all his relations.

CHAP. VIII.

The Hiſtory of Miſs Byron, *who is reſcued by Sir* Charles *from the Attempts of Sir* Hargrave Pollexfen, *who afterwards ſent him a Challenge, which he refuſes to comply with, yet behaves with great Dignity.*

WE ſhall now leave Sir Charles to bring the reader acquainted with an accompliſhed young lady, who will engage his attention in the following part of this work. Miſs Harriet Byron had united in her face the moſt enchanting beauty, grace, and expreſſion ; ſhe had a heart equally pure and open, and a noble mind legible in her lovely and expreſſive countenance. This lady lived at Selbyhouſe, in Northamptonſhire, and was the delight, the pride of her relations, and the admiration of all who either ſaw or converſed with her. She was brought to London by her aunt Reeves, who had paid a viſit to her relations ; and here, as well as in the country, had ſeveral admirers, among whom was Sir Hargrave Pollexfen, a gay, proud, and conceited fop, with a handſome perſon, and an eſtate of 8000l. a year. The Baronet had been accidentally in her company when ſhe enlivened the converſation with the moſt agreeable ſallies of wit ; and afterwards, waiting upon her at Mrs. Reeves's, made an open declaration of his paſſion in the preſence of her uncle and aunt ; on which Miſs Harriet frankly told him, ſhe thanked him for his good opinion, but could not encourage his addreſſes. He appeared amazed at this declaration, and repeating, *cannot encourage my addreſſes !*

F

said, he had been assured her affections were not engaged, but that surely it must be a mistake. She desired to know if it was a necessary consequence, that the woman must be engaged, who could not receive the addresses of Sir Hargrave Pollexfen? Why, madam, as to that, said he, I don't know what to say; —— but to a man of my fortune, and I hope not absolutely disagreeable, either in person or temper, of some rank in life,——what, madam, if you are as much in earnest as you pretend, can be your objections? We can't, said she, all like the same person. Women are said to be very capricious, and, perhaps, I am so; but there is a something, we can't always say what, that attracts or disgusts us. *Disgusts!* madam,——*Disgusts!* Miss Byron, cried he. I hope in general——Sir, she returned, I dare say nineteen women out of twenty would think themselves favoured by the addresses of Sir Hargrave Pollexfen. You, Sir, may have more merit, perhaps, than the man I may happen to like better; but pardon me, Sir, you don't hit my fancy. If pardon depends upon my breath, cried he, let me die if I do!—— *Not hit your fancy*, madam, looking upon himself all round, *not hit your fancy*, madam! In short, the Baronet, provoked at the thought of her rejecting so accomplished a person as himself, behaved with great insolence, charging her with pride, ingratitude, and cruelty; when Miss Byron, being unwilling to stay to be insulted, begged his excuse, and hastily withdrew.

Sir Hargrave soon after paid her another visit, and having apologized for his former behaviour, made vehement professions of love, offered to make her large settlements, and told her, that she should prescribe to him in every thing. To which she answered as before; but on his

infifting upon knowing her reafons for refufing him, fhe
frankly told him, it was with fome reluctance that fhe
owned her not having that opinion of his morals, that
fhe muft have of thofe of the man on whom fhe muft
build her hopes of prefent happinefs, and on whofe guid-
ance entruft her future. Sir Hargrave ftormed, repeating,
My morals, madam ! *You have no opinion of my morals,*
madam ! and then fhewing feveral menacing airs, ab-
ruptly departed.

As this young lady had never before been in London,
Lady Betty Williams, a near relation to Mr. Reeves, infifted on Mifs Byron's accompanying her to a ball at the
Opera-houfe, in the Haymarket, and providing her with
a drefs ; and as fhe would take no denial, fhe with reluctance complied. Mr. Reeves was a Hermit, Mrs. Reeves
a Nun, Lady Betty an Abbefs, and Mifs Byron an Ar-
cadian Princefs. She wore a white Paris-net cap, glitter-
ing with fpangles, and enriched by a chaplet of artificial
flowers, with a fmall white feather on the left fide, and
her hair hung down in natural ringlets, fhading her neck.
She had a kind of waiftcoat of blue fattin, trimm'd with
filver point d'Efpagne, the fkirts edged with filver fringe :
this waiftcoat was faftened clofe to her waift by filver
clafps, with a fmall taffel at each ; and all was fet off
with bugles and fpangles. A fcarf of white Perfian filk
was faftened to her fhoulders, and flew loofe behind.
Her petticoat was of blue fattin, trimmed and fringed
like the waiftcoat. She had bracelets on her arms, and
a Venetian mafk. Mifs Byron took no pleafure in the
place, for the fhoals of fools that fwarmed around her.
The glitter of her drefs, which attracted the eyes of the
company, filled her with confufion, while their infipid and

abfurd behaviour made her frequently defpife both herfelf and them.

They ftaid till about two in the morning, when Mr. Reeves conducted her to her chair, and faw her in it, before he attended Lady Betty and his wife unto theirs ; but obferved, that neither the chair nor the chairmen were thofe that brought her ; on which he afked the reafon of it, and was told by her fervant, who had been hired only a few days before, that the chairmen had been inveigled away to drink, and that after having waited two hours for them, he had hired a chair to fupply their place.

The chair moved off with her fervant, carrying his lighted flambeau before it. The chairmen had not gone a great way, when fhe calling out, they ftopped, and her fervant afked her commands. Where am I, William ? faid fhe. Juft at home, madam, he anfwered, and on her obferving, that they muft have come a roundabout way, told her, they had done fo on purpofe to avoid the croud of coaches and chairs. They then proceeded forwards ; but foon after, in drawing the curtains, fhe found herfelf in the open fields, and prefently after the lights put out ; on which fhe pierced the air with her cries, till her ftrength was exhaufted. She was at laft taken out in fits, and, on recovering her fenfes, found herfelf on a bed with three women about her ; one at her head holding a bottle to her nofe, which was fore with hartfhorn, and the room was filled with the ftrong fmell of burnt feathers. Where am I ? who are you, madam ? fhe cried. No harm is intended you, faid the eldeft of them ; for you are to be made one of the happieft women upon earth. We would not be concerned in a bad action. I hope not, I hope not, fhe returned. You feem to be a mother, thefe young gentlewomen, I prefume, are your daughters. Save me from ruin, I befeech you, madam——Save me from ruin, as you would thefe your daughters. This muſt be the vile contrivance of Sir Hargrave Pollexfen. Is it not ? is it not ? Tell me, I beg you to tell me.

Mifs Byron then rifing, fat on the fide of the bed ; when Sir Hargrave inſtantly entered. She fcreamed out, and he threw himſelf at her feet ; but finding that the women could hardly keep her out of a fit, retired. On her reviving, fhe begged and offered rewards to induce them to facilitate her efcape ; but fhe had fcarce begun to fpeak before Sir Hargrave returned, and haughtily bade her not needlefsly terrify herſelf, ordering the women to withdraw. As they went out, fhe rufhed forward, and followed the foremoſt of the daughters into the parlour, and then finking on her knees, clafped her arms about her, crying, O fave me ! fave me ! Sir Hargrave following them, Mifs Byron kneeled to him, crying, If you have any compaffion, let me now, I befeech you, Sir, experience your mercy. The women again walked out, and he anſwered, I have entreated you, madam, and on my knees too, to fhew me mercy ; but you would fhew me none. Kneel if you will, the tables are now turned. Barbarous man ! faid fhe, rifing from her knees ; but her fpirits immediately fubfiding, fhe added, Don't be cruel, Sir Hargrave, I befeech you ; I never was cruel to any body : you know I was civil to you. Yes, you called me no names, and I call you none. Sweet creature, added he, your very terror is beautiful ! I can enjoy your terror, madam ! Then offering to kifs her, fhe turned afide her head, on which he added, *I don't bit your fancy, madam* ! *You don't like my morals,* madam ! Are thefe,

F 2

Sir Hargrave, faid fhe, the means you take to convince
me that I ought to like them ! Well, madam, he returned, you fhall meet with the mercy in me you would not
fhew.   Be mine, madam, I offer you my honeft hand ;
confent to be Lady Pollexfen——no punifhment, I hope !
or take the confequence.   Take my life, Sir, faid fhe,
but my hand and my heart are my own ; they never
fhall be feparated.   You can't fly me, madam, returned
he ; you are fecurely mine, and mine fhall be ftill more
fecurely.   Don't provoke me, don't make me defperate.
Then throwing his arms about her, fhe was terrified, and
cried out ; when inftantly entered one of the daughters,
crying, Good Sir ! did not you fay you would be honourable ?   The mother following her in, faying, Sir ! Sir !
in my houfe——What a plague, cried he, do you come
in for ?   I thought you knew your own fex better than to
mind a woman's fqualling.   Dear, bleffed, bleffed woman ! cried the lady, frantic with mingled terror and joy,
to find herfelf in better hands than fhe expected ; protect
me ! fave me ! Indeed I have not deferved this treacher-
ous treatment.   Nay, dear lady, faid the women, if Sir
Hargrave will make you his true and lawful wife, there
can be no harm done, furely.   Then turning to him, fhe
told him the gentleman was waiting.

At this inftant entered a horrid looking clergyman ;
he was a tall, big-boned, fplay-footed man, in a fhabby
gown, a wig equally fhabby, with a huge red pimpled
face, and a great red nofe.   He held a dog's eared com-
mon-prayer book in his hand, opened at the page of
matrimony.   But paying little attention to his horrid
vifage, fhe pufhed by Sir Hargrave, turning him half-
round, and making the woman of the houfe totter ; then

throwing herself at the clergyman's feet, Good, dear, reverend Sir, cried she, save a poor creature, basely trick-ed away from her friends.—Save me from violence! don't give your aid to sanctify a base action! The man snuffled his answer, and opening his pouched mouth, the tobacco hung about his great yellow teeth ; when taking her clasped hands, Rise, madam ! said he. Don't kneel to me. No harm is intended you. Who is that gen-tleman in the silver-laced cloaths ? He is Sir Hargrave Pollexfen, Sir, said she ; a wicked, a very wicked man. O madam, returned he, a very honourable man ! bowing to Sir Hargrave. Then asking her name, and she telling it to him, Sir Hargrave seized her hand, and the snuffling priest began, *Dearly beloved*——The lady was perfectly frantic, and crying, Read no more ! read no more ! dashed the book out of his hand, adding, I beg your pardon, Sir ; but you must read no further. I am basely betrayed. I can't, I won't be his. Proceed, proceed, Sir, said Hargrave, taking her hand by force ; virago as she is, I will own her my wife. Again snuffled the min-ister, *Dearly beloved.* She stamped, crying, No dearly beloved's ! while Sir Hargrave held her struggling hand, and the minister proceeded, *We are gathered together in the sight of God.* I adjure you, Sir Hargrave, in the same tremendous name, to stop all further proceedings. Take my life, but my hand shall never be joined with yours. Proceed, Doctor, pray Doctor, proceed, said the vile Sir Hargrave. When the day dawns she'll be glad to own her marriage. Proceed at your peril, Sir, said she. If you are really a minister of God, don't proceed. Don't make me desperate. Then turning to the window, she added, Madam, you are a mother, and have given

me room to hope you are a good woman ; look upon me
as if I was one of thofe your daughters.——Could you
fee one of them treated thus ? Dear young women, turning to each, can you unconcernedly look on, and fee a
poor creature tricked, betrayed, and thus violently, bafely
treated, and not make my cafe your own ? Speak for
me ! plead for me ! If you are women, plead for me !——
You have a foul to anfwer for. I can die ; but never,
never will be his ! The young women wept, and the
mother being moved, defired they might talk to the lady
by themfelves. This was granted, when retiring into
another room, they pleaded Sir Hargrave's great eftate,
his handfome perfon, his honourable love, and their being
unable to fave her from worfe treatment. On the other
hand, Mifs Byron pleaded her invincible averfion, and
contempt of riches, crying, How, not able ! Is not this,
ladies, your own houfe ? Cannot you raife your neighbours ? Before the week is out, I will order a thoufand
pounds to be paid into your hands. I pledge my honour
for the payment——A thoufand pounds, dear ladies, only
to fave me, and fee me fafe to my friends ?

At this moment Sir Hargrave entered, and, with a
malicious look, defired the young women to go to bed,
and leave the perverfe beauty to him. He called her
cruel and ungrateful, fwearing, that if fhe would not permit him to exalt her into Lady Pollexfen, he would
humble her. She would be greatly hurt indeed, cried he,
to be the wife of a man of my fortune and confequence !
But I'll bring down her pride. What the devil am I to
creep, beg, and entreat only for a wife ?——But, madam,
added he, with a fneer, perhaps you'll be mine upon
certain terms.

The mother and youngeft daughter were then led by Sir Hargrave to the door, the eldeft following them, while Mifs Byron entreated them not to go ; and when they did, made an attempt to follow them ; but Sir Hargrave, in fhutting them out, gave her a dreadful crufh with the door, fhe being half in and half out ; her nofe gufhed out with blood ; her ftomach was much preffed, and one of her arms bruifed : fhe fcreamed, and he appeared frighted ; but fhe inftantly recovering herfelf, cried out, fhe hoped he had killed her ; and throwing herfelf into a chair, repeated, So, fo you have killed me. Well, I hope you are now fatisfied. I forgive you ; only leave me to my own fex. She was in violent pain, her head fwam, her eyes failed her, and fhe fainted away. Sir Hargrave, filled with confternation, ran about the room, calling upon God to have mercy upon him, and having let in the women, they lamented over her, and faid fhe had death in her face. The Baronet, in the midft of his horror, feized her bloody handkerchief, and faying it fhould not appear againft him, ftepped into the next room, and thruft it into the fire, by which was fitting the minifter and his helper, over fome burnt brandy. O gentlemen, faid he, nothing can be done to-night. Take this, giving them money ; the lady is in a fit ; I wifh you well home. They, however, propofed to fit in the chimney-corner till peep of day ; but the women fearing fhe would not recover, one of them ran in, and declared fhe was dead, on which, calling for a dram, they fnatched up their hats and fticks and hurried away.

On Mifs Byron's coming to herfelf, fhe found nobody with her but the three women. She was in a cold fweat, and as there was no fire in the room, they conducted her into the parlour which the two men had left, and she being hardly able to ftand, placed her in an elbow chair, and chafed her temples with Hungary water. Soon after the mother and eldeft daughter left her, and went to Sir Hargrave, and the youngeft being at length called out, the Baronet entered, took a chair and fat down by Mifs Byron, who ftill felt a violent pain in her ftomach and arm. At laft the lady breaking filence, faid, Have you done well, Sir Hargrave, to commit fuch violence on one who never did nor thought to injure you ? In what diftraction have you involved my coufin Reeves ! She ftopped, and he continued filent, she refumed, Thefe feem to be honeft people, and I hope you only defign to terrify me. Your bringing me into no worfe company affures me that you meant better——Devils all ! interrupted he. She againft ftopped, but foon added, I forgive you, Sir, the pain you have given me.——But as foon as day breaks, I'll get the women to let my coufin Reeves—— Up he ftarted, crying, Mifs Byron, you are a woman, a true woman, holding up his clenched hand. Then after a fhort paufe, you are the moft confummate hypocrite that I ever knew in my life. She was filent and trembled. Damn'd fool ! Afs ! Blockhead ! Woman's fool ! I could curfe myfelf for fending away the parfon ! But your hypocrify, madam, fhall be of no fervice to you. What I failed in here, fhall be done elfewhere. She wept, but could not fpeak. Can't you go into fits again ? cried he, with a fneering air. God deliver me, prayed she to herfelf, from this madman's hands. She then ftood up, and the candle ftanding near the glafs, faw herfelf in the habit, to which she had hitherto paid little attention. Pray, Sir Hargrave, faid she, let me beg you to terrify me no farther. I will forgive what is paſt, and conſider it as a proper puniſhment for my conſenting to be thus marked for a vain and fooliſh creature. Your abuſe, Sir, allow me to ſay, is low and unmanly ; but in the light of a puniſhment I will confeſs I deſerve it. Let my puniſhment end here, and I'll thank and forgive you with all my heart. Your fate is determined, ſaid he ; and the ſervant maid giving him a capuchin, he repeated, Your fate is determined, madam.——Here, put this on.—— Now fall into fits again !——Put this on. She begged, prayed, and would have kneeled to him, but in vain ; the capuchin was put on, whether ſhe would or no ; and being afterwards muffled up in a man's cloak, in ſpite of all her prayers, ſtruggles, and reſiſtance, he lifted her into a chariot and ſix, which came up to the door.

The chariot was attended by ſeveral men on horſeback, among whom was her own ſervant, and Sir Hargrave ſtepping in, ſaid to him, If you meet with impertinents, you know what to ſay ; and on her ſcreaming out, he upbraidingly cried, Scream on, my dear, and barbarouſly mocked her, imitating the bleating of a ſheep : then rearing himſelf up, cried, with an air of triumph, Now am I Lord of Miſs Byron ! At their firſt ſetting out ſhe once or twice cried out for help, when pretending ſhe would catch cold, he tied a handkerchief over her face and mouth ; and muffling her up in the cloak, leaned againſt her with his whole weight, holding both her hands with one of his, while his other arm, being thrown round her, kept her on her ſeat. On her calling out for help at the approach of paſſengers, ſhe heard one of the men repreſent Sir Hargrave as the beſt of huſbands, and herſelf as the worſt of wives. Thus every glimmering ray of hope vaniſhed from the poor lady's mind.

Sir Charles expecting Lord and Lady L———, who were returning from Scotland, had been at that Nobleman's seat at Colnebrook, where he had left his sister Charlotte, to see every thing but in order against their arrival, and was coming to town in his chariot and six, when meeting Sir Hargrave's chariot, the coachmen seemed to dispute the way. Sir Hargrave looking out, to see what was the matter, Miss Byron pushed the handkerchief from her mouth and eyes, and cried out, Help! help! for God's sake. Sir Charles ordered his coachman to stop, and Sir Hargrave damning his coachman, called out, Drive on when I bid you. The lady again cried out for help, when Sir Charles ordered his servants on horseback to stop the postillion of the other chariot, and bid Sir Hargrave's coachman proceed at his peril. Sir Hargrave, with dreadful execrations, continued calling out on the contrary side of the chariot to that Sir Charles was on : upon which Sir Charles alighting, walked round to the other side, and the lady endeavouring to cry out, he observed Sir Hargrave struggle to put the handkerchief over her mouth, when she seeing the stranger, spread out both her hands, repeating, For God's sake !—Sir Hargrave Pollexfen, by the arms, said, Sir Charles, I am afraid you are engaged in a very bad affair. I am Sir Hargrave Pollexfen, and carrying away a fugitive wife.—Your own wife, Sir Hargrave ? Yes, said he, swearing, and she was going to elope from me, at a damn'd masquerade. See, drawing aside the cloak, I detected her in the very dress ! O no ! no ! no ! said the Lady. Proceed, coachman, cried Sir Hargrave, and cursed and swore. Let me ask the Lady a question, Sir Hargrave. You are impertinent, Sir, said the villain, who the devil are you ? Are you, madam, Lady Pollexfen.? returned Sir Charles. O no ! no ! no ! repeated fhe.

Inftantly two of Sir Charles's fervants rode up to him, and a third held the head of the horfe on which the poft-illion fat. Three of Sir Hargrave's approached on their horfes, but appeared afraid of coming too near. Have an eye on thofe fellows, faid Sir Charles, fome bafe work is on foot. Then addreffing Sir Hargrave's coachman, who lafhed his horfes, he cried, Sirrah, proceed at your peril ; while Sir Hargrave, curfing and threatening him, ordered him to drive over all that oppofed him. Sir Charles then turning to the Lady, faid, madam, will you—O Sir, Sir, Sir, cried fhe, relieve me ! help me for God's fake ! I am in a villain's hands ! Vilely tricked into a villain's hands ! Help ! help ! for God's fake ! Sir Hargrave then drew his fword, and called upon his fervants to fire at all that dared to oppofe his paffage. My fervants, faid Sir Charles, have fire-arms as well as yours, and will not difpute my orders. Don't provoke me to give the word. Will you, madam, put yourfelf into my pro-tection—O yes, yes, Sir, faid fhe, with all my heart !

At this inftant Sir Charles opened the chariot door, when Sir Hargrave making a pafs at him, Take that, fcoundrel ; but Sir Charles being aware of the thruft, put it by, though the fword raked his fhoulder. His own fword was in his hand, but undrawn, and the chariot door remaining open, he feized Sir Hargrave by the col-lar, before he could recover from the pafs he had made, and with a jerk laid him under the hind wheel of the chariot ; then wrenching his fword from him, he fnapped it, and threw away the two pieces. Sir Hargrave's mouth and face were inftantly covered with blood, they being

G

hurt by the pummel of Sir Charles's fword, and one of his legs, in the fprawling, getting between the fpokes of the chariot wheel, Sir Charles charged his coachman not to ftir for his mafter's fake.

Notwithftanding the diforder of Mifs Byron's mind, fhe had difengaged herfelf from the man's cloak. Sir Charles was ftruck with her beauty, but ftill more with her terror. He then offered his hand, but inftead of accepting it, fhe threw herfelf into his arms ready to faint, on which he carried her round Sir Hargrave's horfes, and feating her in his own chariot, affured her that fhe was now in honourable hands, and that he would carry her to his fifter, a young lady of virtue and honour; when fhutting the door, he entreated her to banifh her fears, for he would attend her in a moment. Sir Hargrave's men had fled, and Sir Charles's fervants, having purfued them a little way, were returning to fupport their mafter, when, bidding one of them tell Sir Hargrave his name, he ftepped back to his chariot, where, through terror, fhe was funk down to the bottom, and at his approach, could only fay, Save me! fave me! Sir Charles lifted her on the feat, and giving her all the confolation poffible, carried her to his fifter's.

Mifs Charlotte was fo much furprifed at her brother's unexpected return, and fo affected at the diforder ftill vifible in the lady's countenance, that fhe at firft gave little attention to her drefs; and hearing Sir Charles, in a very tender manner, affure her of his and his fifter's kindeft protection, fhe ftepped up to her, and faluting her, bid her thrice welcome to that houfe. Mifs Byron, too much humbled by her diftrefs, threw herfelf on her knees to Mifs Charlotte, when Sir Charles and that lady,

raifing her to her feat, You fee before you, madam, faid fhe, a ftrange creature, and looked at her drefs ; but I hope you will believe I am an innocent one. Think not hardly, Sir, added fhe, holding up her clafped hands, of her whom you have fo gereroufly delivered. Think not hardly of me, madam ; the vile, vile man—Sir Charles defired his fifter to mak⌐ it her firft care to raife the fpirits of injured beauty, and her next to take her di-rections, and inform her friends of her fafety, obferving, that fuch an admirable young lady could not be miffed an hour without exciting the fears of all her friends : then fending for an eminent phyfician, and repeating that fhe was in honourable hands, and that his fifter would take pleafure in obliging her, took his leave.

The confternation of Mr. and Mrs. Reeves was exceed-ing great, on their coming home from the mafquerade, and finding that Mifs Byron was not there. They im-mediately fent to Lady Betty's ; but fhe being unable to give them any information, every method they could think of was taken to difcover the place to which fhe was carried, but without effect, till they received a letter from Mifs Charlotte, which informed them that fhe had been cruelly treated, but was now in fafe and honourable hands ; and though fhe was very ill, fhe was better than fhe had been. Mr. Reeves inftantly fet out for Lord L's, taking with him a portmanteau filled with Mifs Byron's cloaths, and there found his lovely coufin ill, but filled with gratitude for the favours fhe received from Sir. Charles and Mifs Charlotte.

As to Sir Hargrave, he was not only much bruifed, but had ftill a greater mortification by his having three of his teeth ftruck out in his fall from the chariot, and his up-per lip cut through, which he was obliged to have fewed up.   He vowed revenge, and was no fooner recovered, than he fent Sir Charles a challenge.   But though Sir Charles was perfectly fkilled in the ufe of all the offenfive weapons, he had refolved never to make ufe of them, except in his own defence.   Senfible that duelling was contrary both to the laws of God and fociety, he vindicated his right to guard his own life, and to fpare himfelf the guilt of murder; yet he juftified what he had done, boldly afferting to Sir Hargrave's face, that was he to find him again guilty of a notorious violation of the laws of humanity and juftice, he would again exert himfelf in attempting to fave injured innocence from the effects of brutality.

Sir Charles and his fifter were charmed with the converfation and engaging qualities of their amiable gueft, and became fo extremely fond of her, as to give her the title of fifter ; and on Lord and Lady L's arrival, after Mifs Byron's return to Mr. Reeves's, they were conducted thither by Sir Charles and Mifs Charlotte, that they might fee and acknowledge their new relation.   Mifs Byron's heart was filled with gratitude to her generous deliverer, whofe virtues were the fubject of her admiration ; and this gratitude foon ripened into love.   The whole family feemed to be actuated by one foul : Sir Charles was the tender friend, as well as the affectionate brother ; and both Lord L. his lady and her fifter, confidered him not only as their brother, but as their better father, glorying in their relation to him as their higheft honour.   Upon every new occafion that called forth his virtues, he was the fubject of their praife ; and as Mifs Byron frequently refided for feveral days together at Lord L—'s feat, fhe was informed of all the circumftances of his life which had come to their knowledge.

C H A P. IX.

Sir Charles's *generous Behaviour to* Mr. Danby's *Nephews and Niece.*

MISS Byron, in one of her vifits to Lord L's, was enjoying with the ladies of Sir Charles's family, all the delights that arife from an unreferved fympathy of foul, when their brother fuddenly fet out for Canterbury without telling them the reafon of his journey. They at firft fuppofed, he was carried thither by love, and Mifs Byron fuffered fome inquietude on that fuppofition ; but they were foon informed of the following particulars : Mr. Danby, the French merchant, whofe life Sir Charles had faved, when in France, being ill, was defirous of dying in his native country, and accordingly landed at Dover ; but being unable to proceed any farther in his way to town than to Canterbury, fent for Sir Charles, and dying there, his body was afterwards brought to London. He had two nephews and a niece, who owed their education to him, to each of whom he had alfo given a thoufand pounds to put the young men out apprentices to merchants of credit, and enable them to make a reputable appearance ; and had given them hopes, that at his death he would leave each of them three thoufand pounds more ; but on the attempt made upon his life by the villains employed by their father, of which they were, however, innocent, he left the bulk of his fortune to Sir Charles, making him executor, and refiduary legatee,

after bequeathing two thoufand pounds to each of the
three ; making fome generous remembrances of three of
his friends in France, and defiring his executor to difpofe
of three thoufand to charitable ufes, either in France or
England, and to what objects he pleafed. Had Sir
Charles ftrictly executed this will, he would have been a
confiderable gainer, as Mr. Danby's effects amounted to
upwards of 30,000l. But though he was a little offended
that neither Mr. Danby's nephews nor his niece attended
the funeral, to which he had invited them, nor were prefent at the opening of the will, though he had fent for
them for that purpofe, he was refolved to make up the
defects occafioned by Mr. Danby's extending his refentment to the innocent, and his having too deep a fenfe of
gratitude for Sir Charles's having faved his life. Sir
Charles, therefore, defired Mr. Sylvefter, their attorney,
who came to excufe their attendance, to advife the young
people to recollect themfelves, as he was difpofed to be
kind to them, and wifhed they would place fuch confidence in him, as to give him a particular account of their
views and profpects.

Their attorney, who was a man of character, was
highly pleafed with Sir Charles, and about two hours after he left him, fent him a note in the names of all his
clients, expreffing their gratitude, and their defire to be
allowed the honour of waiting on him that afternoon ; on
which Sir Charles invited the honeft attorney and his
three clients to fup with him. Sir Charles, at the firft
moment, diffipated all their uneafinefs, and they fat down
together with confidence in each other. After their informing him of their different profpects, he, without
keeping them in fufpenfe, afked what had been their ex-

pectations from their uncle, and their profpects ; and
they having given him an account of their views and de-
figns, he told Mr. Thomas Danby, the eldeft, that befides
his legacy, he might reckon upon 5000l. and accordingly
entered into treaty with his mafter for marrying his niece,
and have a fhare in the bufinefs. He commiffioned Mr.
Edward Danby, on the ftrength of the like additional
fum, to treat about entering into partnerfhip with the
gentleman he had ferved. And you, my good Mifs Danby, faid he, fhall acquaint your favoured admirer, the
merchant's fon, that befides the two thoufand pounds
already yours, you'll have five thoufand pounds more
at his fervice. And if thefe fums don't anfwer your
full purpofe, I expect you'll let me know. I never will
be a richer man than I ought to be ; and you muft inform me what other relations you have, and of their different fituations in life, that I may amend a will made in
a long and painful ficknefs, that might four a difpofition
naturally benevolent. They wept, looked at each other,
wiped their eyes, and wept again ; when Sir Charles,
thinking his prefence painful to them, withdrew to his
ftudy. But foon returning, Do you—do you, cried each
brother to the other ; when Mr. Thomas Danby rifing
to fpeak, Sir Charles told them he faw gratitude in their
countenances. Do you think, added he, my pleafure is
not at leaft equal to yours ? I am fufficiently rewarded in
the confcioufnefs of having endeavoured to make a right
ufe of the power entrufted to me. You will each of you,
I hope, with this capital, be eminent in his particular bufinefs. If I have obliged you, let me recommend each of
you, according to your abilities, and as opportunity may
offer, to raife thofe worthy hearts that are rendered fpirit-

lefs by their calamities. Confider what is done for you, not as the reward of any particular merits in yourfelves; but as to that Providence, which has made it a principal part of your religion to do good ; and let me enjoin you, in all your tranfactions, to remember mercy as well as juftice. The brothers declared, that his example had opened their hearts, which they hoped would never be fhut ; the fifter looked the fame declaration ; and Mr. Sylvefter, raifed with this fcene, faid, with tears in his eyes, that after fo noble an example, he fhould be impatient till he had looked into his affairs, in order to qualify himfelf to do fome little good. Sir Charles, at parting, told the nephews, that he expected to hear from them ; and whether their mafters and they agreed or not, he would take the fpeedieft method of putting them into poffeffion of what they were intitled to, as well by his promife, as by their uncle's will. Their fifter wept, and when Sir Charles preffed her hand at taking leave of her, gratefully returned the preffure, but in a manner fo modeft as fhewed that gratitude had poffeffion of her whole heart, and fet her above the forms of her fex.

CH.A P. X.

Miſs Byron ▓▓▓▓ *to Sir* Charles's *Siſters her Love for their* ▓▓▓▓ *Charles lets her know his per-plexed Situation* ▓▓▓▓ *to* Clementina, *who is greatly diſordered* ▓▓▓▓ *nd he being influenced by a Letter fro*▓▓▓▓*n ſets out for* Italy, *with the Advice* ▓▓▓▓ *riting, and attended by a Surgeon.*

MISS Byron was ▓▓▓▓ ſuch inſtances of diſintereſted goodne▓▓▓▓verer; and Sir Charles's ſiſters, by whom ſhe was tenderly beloved, ob-ſerving the pleaſure with which ſhe liſtened to every thing they ſaid of him, and the delight ſhe took in his conver-ſation, prevailed on her to confeſs the impreſſion he had made on her heart; letting her know, that they wiſhed to acknowledge her as their real ſiſter, and generouſly of-fered their aſſiſtance, in order to diſcover the ſituation of their brother's mind. They knew that he had a high eſteem for Miſs Byron, but could not be certain that he was not under engagements to ſome foreign beauty. They therefore applied for information to the worthy Doctor Bartlett, who was now Sir Charles's chaplain, and was well acquainted with every circumſtance of his life. But this gentleman referred them to their brother; on which they took the firſt opportunity to aſk him whether he had any thought of marriage, and if his heart was in the poſſeſſion of any foreign lady. To this he only anfwered, that he was in a very difficult fituation, and far from being happy. But a few days after, taking Mifs Byron into Lord L———'s ftudy, he gave her the hiftory of the noble Clementina and his frien█████ronymo, referring her, for further particulars, to hi████████ to Dr. Bartlett. She was extremely moved █████████ffecting ftory, admired and pitied the lovely ███████n, a██; every hope of happinefs by an union wit███████being now vanifhed, refolved to ufe her utmoft████████ to conquer her paffion.

Sir Charles, fome da██████████d a vifit to Mifs Byron at her uncle Reev██████, ███████████eing left alone with her, he, with a folen████████████ed her: The laft time I had the honour ████████████ with my good Mifs Byron, I told her a████████████e, which muft raife in fuch a heart as █████████████ compaffion for the nobleft lady on the continent. The ftory did, indeed, affect you; and I am fure you muft have fuffered ftill more from the fame compaffionate goodnefs on the communications made you by Dr. Bartlett. May I be allowed, Madam, to add a few particulars on the fame fubject? for I am defirous to acquaint you, rather than any woman in the world, with all I know myfelf of this melancholy affair. Mifs Byron, with trembling hefitation, anfwered, that the ftory was, indeed, a moft affecting one, and that he would do her an honour in acquainting her with further particulars. Sir Charles then told her, that Clementina's brother the Bifhop had written to entreat, that he would once more vifit Bologna, though the General was againft his coming. He offered to meet him where he pleafed, and to conduct him to Bologna, where his prefence would rejoice every heart. He likewife fhewed her a letter from Mrs. Beaumont, which informed him of many affecting particulars. The noble, yet unhappy Clementina had been hurried from place to place, with the expectation of seeing him, and had afterwards been put into the hands of the Lady Sforza, and her daughter Laurana, who, from interested motives, and envy of her superior qualities, had treated her with the utmost cruelty. Miss Byron wept at reading the affecting particulars of those inhumanities which had broken the spirit of the excellent Lady, while Sir Charles cried out, How insupportable would have been my reflections, did my conscience tell me that I had been the wilful cause of the noble Clementina's calamities ! He also shewed her a letter from Seignior Jeronymo, which informed him that his life was a burden to him, and that he did not think himself in skilful hands, wishing that Sir Charles and himself had been of one country, since the greatest felicity he could now enjoy would be to resign up his life to the great Author of it, in the arms of his dearest friend.

At this instant Mr. Reeves entering the room, Miss Byron walked to the window, and strove to recollect herself. The gentleman soon after withdrew, when Sir Charles coming up to her, My heart bleeds, Sir, said she, for the distresses of your Clementina ; I admire, beyond expression, the greatness of her behaviour, and most sincerely do I lament her distresses. But what is there in the power of man that Sir Charles Grandison cannot do ? You, Sir, have honoured me with the title of sister, and in the tenderness of that relation, permit me to say, that I dread the effects of the General's petulance : I feel for you the pain it must give your humane heart to be once more personally present to the woes of the inimitable lady :

H

but, I am fure, you did not hefitate a moment about leaving
all your friends here, and refolving to hafte over, to try at
leaft what can be done for the noble fufferer. Sir Charles
leading her to her feat, and taking his by her, anfwered,
Ever fince I had the honour of knowing Mifs Byron, I
have confidered her as one of the moft excellent of women. My heart demands an alliance with hers, though
I am in fo perplexed a fituation, that I fcarcely dare truft
myfelf to fpeak on the fubject. From the firft, I called
Mifs Byron my fifter ; but fhe is even more to me than
the deareft fifter ; and whatever may be the accidents of
either fide to bar a further wifh, I afpire to hold a more
tender friendfhip with her ; and this, I hope, fhe will not
deny me, fo long as it fhall be confiftent with her other
attachments.—He paufed, and fhe made an effort to
fpeak, but could not utter a word. He then told her,
that he had wrote to the Bifhop, that he would moft
cheerfully comply with his wifhes, and that as Jeronymo
expreffed himfelf diffatisfied with his furgeons, he only
waited for a fkilful one, who was fettling his affairs, in
order to go with him. Then, inviting Mifs Byron to dine
with him the next day, he took his leave.

. Sir Charles having fettled fome important affairs, particularly the marriage of his fifter Charlotte to Lord
G——, and obtained the opinion of feveral eminent phyficians in writing on Lady Clementina's cafe, he fet out
for Italy, by the way of France, accompanied by Mr.
Lowther, a fkilful furgeon.

CHAP. XI.

Sir Charles *rescues* Sir Hargrave Pollexfen *from the fur-*
ther Resentment of the Persons whom he had injured.
The Reception he meets with from the noble family at
Bologna, *who consent to his marrying the unhappy*
Clementina *on his own Terms ; but when he thinks his*
Happiness secure, she, from a Scruple of Conscience, rejects
him, and entreats him to marry another Lady. *The dif-*
tressful Scenes which followed.

IN his journey to Paris, he was stopped by one of Sir
Hargrave Pollexfen's servants, who gave him a dismal
account that his master and another gentleman had been
attacked by several men, who were at that time murder-
ing them behind a hill at a small distance. Sir Charles,
leaping out of the post-chaise, desired Mr. Lowther's servant to dismount, and getting on his horse, galloped away
with his three servants towards the place. His ears were
soon pierced with the poor wretches cries, and he beheld
two men on horseback, holding the horses of four others,
who had two gentlemen under them, struggling, groaning,
and crying for mercy. Sir Charles, who was a good way
a head of his servants, called to them to spare the gentlemen, and galloping towards the prostrate sufferers, two of
the four quitted them, and mounting, joined the two
other horsemen, advancing to meet him, with a shew of
supporting the two men on foot, who continued laying on
the wretches unmercifully with the butt-end of their

whips. The four men on horfeback, demanded a con-ference, with their piftols in their hands, as Sir Charles alfo had his, advifing him not to provoke his fate by his rafhnefs, and declaring that he was a dead man if he fired. Sir Charles bid them forbear all further violence to the gentlemen, and then he would hear what they had to fay. He then put his piftol into his holfter, and one of his fer-vants coming up, and the two others being at hand, he called out to them not to fire till they had his orders ; and giving him his horfe's reins, leaped down, drew his fword, and advanced towards the two men who were fo cruelly exercifing their whips ; but on his approach, they drew their hangers, and retired to a little diftance. The four men on horfeback joining the two on foot, juft as they were quitting the object of their fury, one of them faid, Forbear, brother, for the prefent, any further violence ; the gentleman fhall be told the caufe. Murder, Sir, faid he, is not intended, nor are we robbers ; thofe you are folicitous to fave, are villains. At this inftant, Sir Charles raifed firft one groaning man, and then the other. Their heads were covered with blood, and they were fore bruifed, that they could not extend their arms to reach their wigs and hats which lay near them. By this time the men on foot had mounted their horfes, and all fix ftood on their defence ; but one of them was fo furious, that two of the others could fcarce reftrain him, he crying that his vengeance fhould be ftill more complete. At this inftant came up Mr. Lowther, and his fervant in the chaife, each with a piftol in his hand ; and he having, at Sir Charles's defire, examined their wounds, declared that there was no apparent danger of death. On which Sir Charles obferved, that as they had neither attempted to fly, nor been guilty of violence to himſelf, his friend, or ſervants, he was afraid they had reaſon to think themſelves ill uſed by the gentlemen. You, Sir, cried one of them, ſeem to be a man of honour and temper ; we are men of honour as well as you. Our deſign was not to kill the miſcreants, as we told you, but to give them reaſon to remember their villainy as long as they lived, and to put it out of their power ever to be guilty of the like. They have made a vile attempt on a lady's honour at Abbeville, and finding themſelves detected, have endeavoured, by round-about ways, to eſcape the vengeance of her friends. That gentleman has reaſon for being enraged, ſince he is the lady's huſband ; that and that are her brothers. The villains have not yet been puniſhed as they deſerve ; but let them aſk on their knees this gentleman's pardon, pointing to the huſband, and promiſe never more to come within two leagues of Abbeville, and we will leave them in your protection. Sir Charles then turning towards Sir Hargrave and his companion, ſaid, Gentlemen, if you have done wrong, you ought not to ſcruple aſking pardon ; but if you know yourſelves to be innocent, though I would be loth to riſque the lives of my friend and ſervants, my countrymen ſhall not make ſo undue a ſubmiſſion. The wretches inſtantly kneeled ; and the others civilly ſaluting Sir Charles and Mr. Lowther, rode off, to the great joy of the two delinquents, who again kneeled to their deliverers, pouring forth bleſſings on the man whoſe life one of them had ſo lately ſought, and in whoſe preſervation he had ſuch reaſ to rejoice. Sir Hargrave's poſt-chaiſe now coming up, he and his companion were with difficulty lifted into it, while Sir Charles and Mr. Lowther went into theirs, and

H 2

being only at a fmall diſtance from Paris, they proceeded
, to that city in company.

Sir Charles was met at Parma by the Biſhop and Father Mareſcotti, where he found them at the palace of the
Count of Belvedere.   They all expreſſed great joy at ſee-
ing him; but told him, on his enquiring after the Barone
Jeronymo, that he was alive, and that was all; however,
the ſight of his friend would be a cordial to his heart. As
to Clementina, her bodily health was greatly impaired,
and they bad little hopes of the recovery of her mind.
They both regretted that ſhe had been denied the requeſt-
ed interview at his departure, and were convinced, that if
it had been granted, and ſhe had been left to Mrs. Beaumont's friendly care, they might have expected a happy,
iſſue.   The next day they ſet out for Bologna, and the
Count of Belvedere accompanying them about half way,
found an opportunity to mention to Sir Charles his unabated paſſion for Clementina, and that he had lately made
offers to marry her, notwithſtanding the diſorder of her
mind, ſince he flattered himſelf that her cure was not im-
poſſible.

Sir Charles, on his arrival at Bologna, haſted to the
Barone, who, the moment he ſaw him, cried, Do I once
more behold my friend, my Grandiſon ? Let me embrace
my deareſt friend. Now, now, I have lived long enough;
and bowing his head on his pillow, his countenance ſhone
with pleaſure, in ſpite of his pain. The Biſhop then led
him to the Marquis and Marchioneſs, when his reception
from the former was kind, but from his lady, it was that
of a mother to a long abſent child. She told him, ſhe
had ever eſteemed him her fourth ſon, and now he had
brought over with him a ſurgeon of experience, and advice in writing of eminent phyſicians of his country, the

obligations he had laid on their whole family were too great ever to be returned. They received Mr. Lowther with great politenefs, and recommended their Jeronymo to his beft fkill. His two furgeons were fent for, and Sir Charles having given them Mr. Lowther's charaĉter, prefented him to them, and they informed him of their method of proceeding. The fame evening Mr. Lowther affifted at the dreffings, and in fo eafy and gentle a manner fuggefted an alteration, that the gentlemen came readily into it. The family were now delighted with Mr. Lowther, and flattered themfelves with the hopes of the Barone's recovery.

When Sir Charles had been a few days at Bologna, the Lady Clementina was brought thither by the General and his Lady, to whom he had lately been married. The General could never bear the thought that Sir Charles, an Englifh proteftant, fhould be thought of fuch confequence to his fifter's happinefs; hence he had always been his enemy : he therefore now expreffed himfelf with coldnefs on his coming over, and treated him with contempt. This behaviour Sir Charles refented, and with a noble fuperiority of behaviour obliged him to banifh his unjuft fufpicions, and at length to grant him his efteem. The lady Clementina feemed the piĉture of filent woe ; fhe neither knew nor paid the leaft attention to her mother, of whom fhe had never before been unmindful ; hence it was refolved to revive her attention, by introducing her in a full affembly, in which Sir Charles was prefent. Being before told that he was arrived, fhe entered, having only Camilla, her woman, with her fervant Laura attending. Her motion was flow and folemn ; her robes were black and flowing ; her dejeĉted face was half covered by a veil of black gauze, and her eyes were caſt on the ground. Sir Charles aroſe from his ſeat, ſat down, and roſe again irreſolute, not knowing what he did, or what to do. She approached the table round which the company ſat, but with her eyes caſt down, and more than half cloſed : ſhe then turned towards the window. Here, here, madam, ſaid Camilla, leading her to a chair that had been placed for her between the Marchioneſs and the General's Lady. She ſat down. Her mother wept, as did alſo the General's Lady ; and her father ſobbing, turned his head aſide. Her mother then took her hand, ſaying, My love, look around you ; but ſhe took no notice. The General, grieved and impatient, aroſe ; ſtepped to her ; and hanging over her ſhoulder, cried, My deareſt ſiſter, look upon us all. See your father, mother, ſiſter, and every body in tears. If you love us, ſmile upon us ; when lifting up her eyes to him, ſhe tried to ſmile ; but ſuch a ſolemnity had taken poſſeſſion of her features, that her ſmile appeared the ſmile of woe. The Marquis riſing from his ſeat, with his handkerchief at his eyes, cried, ſweet creature ! never, never let me ſee again ſuch a ſmile as that. It is here, added he, laying his hand on his boſom. Obliging ſiſter, ſaid the General ; ſee Father Mareſcotti is in tears, (he ſat by Sir Charles) pity his grey hairs ! She caſt her eyes that way, and ſaw Sir Charles greatly affected. She ſtarted. She looked again ; again ſtarted, reddening and growing pale by turns. She roſe, then threw her arms about Camilla, who ſtood by her, crying, O Camilla ! then gave way to a violent burſt of tears. Sir Charles was ſpringing to her, and before them all would have claſped her in his arms, but the General ſtopping him, ſaid, Dear Grandi-

fon, keep your feat. If Clementina remembers her Englifh tutor, fhe will once more welcome you to Bolog- na. O Camilla, faid fhe, faithful good Camilla ! now at laft you have told me the truth ! It is, it is he, hiding her face in Camilla's bofom. She then, fupported by the Marchionefs and the General's Lady, turned towards the door ; but S Charles coming up to her, fhe ftopped, and faying, Ah, hevalier, reclined her head on her moth- er's bofom, feeming ready to faint. He took her hand, and kneeling, preffed it to his lips, crying, Forgive me, ladies, forgive me, Lady Clementina ! His foul overflow- ing with tendernefs, he could fay no more ; he therefore arofe. She moved on to the door, and there turned her head, ftraining to look at him till fhe was out of the room, Sir Charles ftanding like a ftatue.

After this, many tender interviews paffed between Sir Charles and Clementina. All the family repeatedly ufed the moft earneft perfuafions to induce Sir Charles to change his religion ; but thofe proving ineffectual, they confented to give him Clementina on the conditions he himfelf had propofed : The daughters were, therefore, to be confidered as Italians, they were to be educated in Italy, and to enjoy the great eftate given to Clementina by her two grandfathers, on condition of her marrying ; while the fons, as being proteftants, were to be educated in En- gland, and provided for by their father. Meanwhile, Sir Charles's joy was damped by the grief of the Count of Belvedere, who arrived at Bologna, paid him feveral vifits ; and being weary of life, ftrove but in vain, to pre- vail on Sir Charles to meet him without the city gates, protefting that while he had life, Clementina fhould not be his.

The whole family having confented to Sir Charles's

union with Clementina, and the marriage articles being settled, it was imagined she would have received his hand with tranfport : but now a fudden thoughtfulnefs took poffeffion of her mind, and she fpent a confiderable time in writing. On Sir Charles being introduced to her, she received him with tears, fighs, and trembling hefitation ; and having put a paper into his hand, ⬛ed, Leave me, leave me ; then retiring to her clofet, shut the door, and fell on her knees ; when Sir Charles, to avoid hearing fighs which pierced his heart, walked into the next room, where he found her mother and Camilla, who inftantly went to her ; when opening the paper, he was aftonished at finding that it contained the moft earneft perfuafions to banish all thoughts of being united to her by marriage, urged with all the tendernefs of mind influenced by pity, and overflowing with love and gratitude ; the fubftance of which is as follows :

O thou whom my heart loveth ; my tutor, my brother, my friend ; feek me not to marriage. Thy foul was ever moft dear to Clementina ; whenever I meditated the gracefulnefs of thy perfon, I reftrained my eye, I checked my fancy, by meditating on the fuperior graces of thy mind. And is not that foul, thought I, to be faved ? Dear, obftinate, and perverfe ! And shall I bind my foul to a foul allied to perdition ?—O thou moft amiable of men ! how can I be fure, that were I thine, thou wouldft not draw me after thee, by thy love, by thy fweet- nefs of manners, by thy condefcending goodnefs ? I who once thought a heretic the worft of beings, have been al- ready lead by the amiablenefs of thy piety, by the univer- fality of thy charity, to think more favourably of all her- etics for thy fake. Of what force could be the advice

of the moſt pious confeſſor, were thy condeſcending goodneſs and ſweet perſuaſion to be exerted, to melt a heart
wholly thine ? O thou, whom my ſoul loveth, ſeek not
to entangle me by thy love ! Were I to be thine, my duty
to thee would miſlead me from that I owe to my God,
and make me more than temporally unhappy ; for, canſt
thou, can I be indifferent in theſe high matters ? Haſt
thou not ſhewn me that thou canſt not ? And ſhall I not
be inſtructed by thy example ? Shall a wrong religion
have a force and efficacy upon thee, which a right one
cannot have upon me ? O thou moſt amiable of men !
ſeek not to entangle me by thy love. But doſt thou indeed love me, or is it owing to thy generoſity, thy noble-
neſs, thy compaſſion for a creature, who aiming to be
great, like thee, could not ſuſtain the effort ? I know
thou loveſt Clementina ; it is her pride to think thou doſt.
But ſhe is not worthy of thee. Yet let thy heart own
that thou loveſt her ſoul, her immortal ſoul, and her future peace. In that wilt thou ſhew thy love, as ſhe has
endeavoured to ſhew hers. Thou art all magnanimity ;
thou canſt ſuſtain the effort to which ſhe was unequal.
Make ſome other woman happy, but let it not be an
Italian.

　　O thou whom my ſoul loveſt ! let me try the greatneſs
of thy love, and the greatneſs of thy ſoul, by thy endeavours to ſtrengthen, and not to impair a reſolution, which,
after all, it will be in thy power to make me break or
keep ! but my brain wounded, my health impaired, can
I expect a long life ? And ſhall I not endeavour to make
the cloſe of it happy ? But, O my friends, what can we
do for this great and good man, in return for his goodneſs
to two of your children ? Theſe obligations lie heavy upon

I

my heart. Yet who knows not his magnanimity ? Divine, almoſt divine Philanthropiſt, canſt thou forgive me ? I know thou canſt. Thou haſt the ſame notions that I have of the brevity and vanity of this world's glory, and of the duration of that to come! If I have the courage, the reſolution to ſhew thee this paper, do thou enable me, by thy great example, to complete the conqueſt of myſelf ; and do not put me upon taking advantage of the generoſity of my honoured friends—Yet, after all, it muſt be, let me own, in thy choice, (for I cannot bear to be thought ungrateful to ſuch exalted merit,) to add what name thou pleaſeſt to that of Clementina.

At reading this paper, Sir Charles was amazed, confounded, and filled with admiration at the angelic ſoul of this lady. He threw himſelf on a couch, without thinking of Camilla, who ſat in the window. Clementina rang, Camilla haſted to her. He ſtarted as ſhe paſſed him, and aroſe ; but on her return, ſhe rouſed him from the ſtupefaction with which he was ſeized. O Sir, cried ſhe, my poor lady fears your anger ; ſhe fears, yet hopes to ſee you. Haſte, haſte, and ſave her from fainting. He ran in. The admirable lady met him half way, and throwing herſelf at his feet, ſaid, Forgive, forgive the creature that muſt be miſerable, if ſhe has offended you. He attempted to raiſe her, but ſhe cried, ſhe would not riſe till he had forgiven her. He then kneeled to her as ſhe kneeled, and claſping her in his arms, cried, Forgive you, madam ! O inimitable woman ! Can you forgive me for having preſumed, and for ſtill preſuming, to hope to call ſuch an angel mine ! Being ready to faint, ſhe threw her arms about Sir Charles, to ſupport herſelf. Camilla held her ſalts to her noſe, and ſhe again repeated, Am I, am I forgiven ! Say that I am. Forgive you, Madam ! he returned, you have done nothing that wants forgiveneſs ! I admire your greatneſs of mind. What you wiſh, bid me be, and that I will be. Riſe, moſt excellent of human creatures ! Sir Charles then raiſing her, led her to a chair, and involuntarily kneeled on one knee with both her hands in his, and looked up to her with eyes filled with love and reverence. Camilla had haſted to the Marchioneſs, crying, O Madam ! ſuch a ſcene ! haſten up, haſten up. They will faint in one another's arms. The Marchioneſs ran after Camilla, and found them thus kneeling. Dear Chevalier, cried ſhe, for the ſake of my child's head, reſtrain your grateful rapture ! O madam, ſaid he, riſing and taking one of her hands, glory in your daughter : you always loved and admired her ; you will now glory in her, ſhe is an angel. Permit me, madam, added he, looking at Clementina, to preſent this paper to the Marchioneſs. He then gave it her, ſaying, Read it, madam, let your Lord, let the Biſhop, let Father Mareſcotti read it. But read it with compaſſion for me, and then direct me what to ſay, what to do ! I reſign myſelf entirely to your direction and theirs ; and to yours, my dear lady Clementina. You ſay you forgive me, Chevalier, ſaid ſhe ; now ſhall I forgive myſelf, God's goodneſs and yours will, I hope, perfectly reſtore me. O Chevalier, love my mind, as yours was ever the object of my love.

Every perſon in the family were aſtoniſhed at this unexpected turn : the Barone pitied his friend, telling him that he could not bear to ſee a mind like his ſubject to the petulance of a brain ſick girl : but none of them imagined ſhe would be able to keep her reſolution ; and to encourage Sir Charles, they reminded him, that she had entirely put herself in his power, by writing that he might add what name he pleafed to that of Clementina. Sir Charles, however, perceived, that her confcience was concerned, and notwithftanding his paffion, he told them, he could not refolve to perfuade her to violate it. Dear Grandifon, faid the Bifhop, taking his hand, how I admire you ! But can you be fo great ? Shall I not, my Lord, he returned, emulate fuch an example fet by a woman ? I came over without any interefted views. I, indeed, confidered myfelf as bound by the conditions to which I had formerly agreed ; but the lady Clementina and your family, as free. If fhe perfifts in her prefent refolution, I will endeavour to acquiefce.

A few days after, the Marchionefs, in Clementina's name, begged of Sir Charles, that he would accept of her on the conditions they themfelves had propofed, and that he would change his religion. Father Marefcotti feconding the motion, would have entreated him on his knees. O Chevalier, faid the Bifhop, how happy is it in your power to make us all ! You will not, I hope, dear Grandifon, faid the Marquis, refufe my daughter. Afk any conditions of us. She fhall be with you in England in a month's time. We will accompany her thither, and ftay till you fhall chufe to return with us. Jeronymo, fobbing, caught his hand, crying, For God's fake, for my fake, for all our fakes, for your foul's fake, my Grandifon, be ours. Let your Jeronymo call you brother. If my tears, if my prayers have weight, faid the Marchionefs, let me call down my child, and fhe fhall give you her hand in our prefence. She thinks, befides her regard for your foul, that fhe ought to infift upon the terms on which we would have confented to make her yours, in gratitude for our compliance with her wifhes. Deareft Grandifon ! rejoined the Bifhop, refufe not my fifter, re-fufe not the affenting Clementina.

They were all filent, with their eyes fixed upon Sir Charles, on which he replied, Refufe lady Clementina, faid you ! How you wound my foul by the fuppofition ! Lady Clementina's generous and condefcending propofal, when I am willing to allow terms to her that fhe will not to me, fhews how important fhe thinks the difference be-tween the two religions ; and I have only to confefs my-felf that the power of refufal lies where it ought. Yet let me add, this company cannot think me too folemn— Were I to live always here, and were convinced that there is no life after this, your commands and Clementina's would be laws to me. But has fhe not the goodnefs to fay in her paper, that I have the fame notions as fhe of the brevity and vanity of this world's glory, and of the duration of that to come. It is hard, very hard, faid the Bifhop, for a man convinced of the truth of his religion, to allow to another of a different perfuafion, what he ex-pects fhould be allowed for himfelf. You, Chevalier, however, can allow it ; and have fuch greatnefs of mind, as to judge favourably of thofe who cannot. I do love you, but fain would I love you more. The Marchionefs wept. My dear love, faid the Marquis, taking her hand, how many tears has this affair coft you ! My heart bleeds to fee you weep. The Chevalier is unworthy of our child, unworthy of the terms we offered him, unworthy of our joint entreaties—He is an invincible man.

Sir Charles being greatly affected, withdrew ; but hav-ing taken two or three turns in the faloon, returned ; on

I 2

which the Marquis coming to him, cried, I am forry——
Not one word of apology, my Lord, faid Sir Charles, in-
terrupting him : I did not withdraw from refentment,
but purely from concern, that in your opinion I' did not
deferve the honour done me by one fo dear to you.——
Think me unhappy, my Lord, and pity me. Principle,
not perverfenefs, influences me ; it does every one prefent, it does the lady above ; and fhall we not allow for
one another, when we are all actuated by the fame motive ? At this the Bifhop threw his arms about Sir
Charles, crying, Generous expanfion of heart !

   Sir Charles now finding that Clementina ftedfaftly per-
fifted in her refo action, defired they would allow him to
make one effort to convince her that fhe might be happy
with him, by endeavouring to remove her fcruples with
refpect to his inviolable honour, and his allowing her the
free exercife of her religion. To this they at length confented, and fhe defiring to fee him, he earneftly pleaded
his having agreed to allow her her chapel, her confeffor,
and her own fervants. He alleged that he might prevail
on her father and mother to give them the pleafure of
their company in their firft journey to England ; and that
the Barone would likewife go with them, and might ob-
tain great benefit from the ufe of the reftorative baths of
his country. He expatiated on the pleafure fhe would receive from the affection of his fifters and their lords, who
would accompany her in her journies to Italy ; and
on the delight with which fhe would every other year
vifit and revifit England and her native country. How
dear, cried he, will you be, in turn, to your old friends
and to your new !——My deareft Clementina ! let me
hear you fay, that you think you can be happy, and yet

blefs me with your love. O how, faid fhe, fhall I guard myfelf againft a voice that is the voice of love !—If I attempt to argue I am loft ! Does not this fhew me, that were I to be yours, I muft be all you wifh ? And then my everlafting peace ! my everlafting happinefs ! O Chevalier ! I doubt not your juftice, your generofity ;· but I fear myfelf :—Seek not, let me repeat, feek not, kindeft of men, to entangle me with your love. Sir Charles, fearing fhe would have fainted, clafped her in his arms ; and fhe returned, Let me, let me cut fhort what I intended to fay, by referring you to my paper, which cannot be anfwered to my fatisfaction. Be my advocate to your own heart, and feek not, deareft of men, to entangle me with your love. Sir Charles then affured her, that whatever it coft him, he would yield to her pleafure, and never urge her again on that fubject, except he was informed by the Bifhop that fhe had changed her mind.

The agitations he had fuffered were fcarcely to be fupported ; and as he found his health affected, he thought it neceffary, both on the noble lady's account and his own, to wean himfelf by abfence. He therefore vifited feveral cities of Italy, and then returned to take his final leave of Bologna. The joy and gratitude of the Marquis, his lady, and her fon, on the recovered intellects of their incomparable daughter ; the pleafing profpect of the recovery of Jeronymo, and their admiration and affection for a perfon to whom they were under fuch great obligations, made them at a lofs how to return the favour he had conferred upon them ; and they entreated him to let them know what return he would accept : on which he, obferved, that the higheft favour he could poffibly receive, would be the honour of a vifit, the next fpring, from that noble family ; by which means, he made no doubt, but that his dear Jeronymo would be perfectly recovered by the ufe of the Englifh baths.. They accepted this propofal with hearts filled with admiration, and Sir Charles, after taking an affecting leave of Clementina and Jeronymo, fet out for England..

C H A P. XII.

Mifs Byron *ftruggles to conquer her Paffion* ; *but* Sir Charles *no fooner returns to* England, *than he pays his Addreffes to her. Their Courtfhip and Marriage.*

DURING his ftay in Italy, he had fent to Dr. Bart-let a particular account of whatever paffed in rela-tion to the noble Clementina ; and thefe letters were conftantly fent by Sir Charles's fifters to Mifs Byron ; who, notwithftanding her love for the writer, had the generofity to admire the lady, who, in a thoufand inftan-ces fhewed the greatnefs of her mind, and the dignity of her fentiments. By fome of thefe letters, Mifs Byron was deprived of all hope of being united to her generous deliverer, who alone had ever made an impreffion on her heart ; fhe however ftrove to acquiefce with chearfulnefs in her lot, and to confider him only as a dear and invalu-able friend, while fhe ftruggled to banifh every idea of his being more nearly related to her ; but the ftruggles with herfelf had fuch an effect, that her health gradually, declined.

On Sir Charles's arrival in his native country, he was received by his family and friends with the warmeft teft-

imonies of joy : but he was extremely alarmed at the
news of Mifs Byron's illnefs ; he therefore took a journey into Northamptonfhire, where that lady lived with
her relations, and paid a vifit to Mrs. Shirley, her grandmother, an elderly lady of a very amiable character ;
when, informing her of his fituation with refpect to
Clementina, he afked, if it was confiftent with her notions of delicacy to give her intereft in his favour ; adding, that if it was, and if Mifs Byron would accept of a
heart that had been thus unaccountably divided, they
would lay him under an obligation that he could only endeavour to return by the utmoft gratitude and affection :
then defiring an anfwer in writing, he left upon the table feveral letters he had received from Jeronymo and
Clementina, with his anfwers, that fhe might fee that
the affair was entirely finifhed between him and that lady, and then took his leave.

Immediately Mrs. Shirley fent for Mifs Byron, Mr.
and Mrs. Selby, with fome other relations ; and having
informed them of the welcome news, they read the letters, which gave them entire fatisfaction ; on which the
old lady wrote to Sir Charles, that they received, as the
higheft honour, the offer he had made of an alliance that
would do credit to families of the firft rank ; and that
it had been their moft ardent wifh, that the man who
had refcued the dear creature might be at liberty to enti-
tle himfelf to her grateful love.

Sir Charles, on receiving this welcome letter, paid his
addreffes to Mifs Byron. She at firft received him with
vifible confufion, but was foon encouraged by his polite
and tender behaviour. He fhewed her another letter
from Jeronymo, in which his dear friend urged him to

set an example to Clementina, by entering into the marriage state ; and informed him, that the noble lady wished for nothing more than to hear of his being happily
married. You see, madam, added he, I am fully free,
with regard to Clementina ; free by her own choice. It
was always Clementina's wish that I would marry, and,
only be careful that my choice should not disgrace her regard for me ; but when she has the pleasure of knowing
the dear lady before me, if I am allowed that honour, she
will confess that my choice has done the highest credit to
the favour she honoured me with. He was silent, and
seemed to expect an answer. The honour, said she,
with much hesitation, of Sir Charles Grandison, no one
ever did, or ever can doubt. I must own—I must confess——Here she paused. What does my dear Miss Byron own ? What confess ? said he. Assure yourself,
madam, of my honour, of my gratitude. Should you
have doubts, speak them. This, Sir, said she, is my confession, the confession of a heart no less sincere than yours,
that I am dazzled and confounded at the superiour merits
of the noble lady you still so justly esteem. I fear not, Sir,
any more than she, your honour, your justice, your indulgent tenderness. Your character, your principles are
full security to the woman who shall endeavour to deserve
that indulgence. But so justly high do I think of the
Lady Clementina's conduct, that I fear it is impossible—
What impossible ? What does my dear Miss Byron fear
is impossible ? Thus kindly urged, returned she, why shall
I not speak all that is in my mind ? The poor Harriet
Byron, when she contemplates the magnanimity of that
excellent lady, fears, that with all her endeavours, she
shall never be able to make the figure to herself that is ne-

ceffary for her tranquillity. This, Sir, is all my fear. Generous, kind, noble Mifs Byron, returned he, in a rapture ; and is this all your fear ? Then muft the man before you be happy. Clementina has acted glorioufly, preferring her religion and her country to all other confiderations ; and fhall I not be doubly bound in gratitude to her fifter's excellence, who not having thefe trials, yet the moft delicate of human minds, fhews in my favour a franknefs of heart which fets her above little forms, and at the fame time a generofity with regard to the merits of another lady, that has few examples ? May my future life be attended with bleffings, in proportion as this grateful heart fhall acknowledge your goodnefs !

Mifs Byron having now before her the profpect of an union with a perfon entitled to her tendereft love, efteem, and gratitude ; a happinefs which fhe had not till this time even dared to hope for ; her heart was oppreffed with the excefs of her joy, and the view of the completion of her higheft hopes filled her with apprehenfions. On Sir Charles's preffing her to name the happy day, her generous concern for the diftreffes of the noble lady made her defire to wait till he had received a letter, in anfwer to one he had wrote, to inform her that he had paid his addreffes to an Englifh lady, who would do honour to his choice. At length this letter arrived, and in it the generous Clementina, in the fulleft terms, expreffed her wifhes that the Englifh lady might make him as happy as fhe herfelf would have endeavoured to have done, had not an infurmountable obftacle intervened ; declaring that fhe wifhed for nothing with greater ardour than to hear of the celebration of their nuptials.

At laft, the happy day was fixed. The relations of

Mifs Byron chofe to have the ceremony performed in as
public a manner as poffible ; and Sir Charles coming into
their meafures, that lady acquiefced, though fhe could
not, without great uneafinefs, think of being expofed, on
this folemn occafion, to the view of a number of fpectators. Sir Charles invited his neareft relations, and thofe
of Mifs Byron were defirous of attending her. On the
morning of the happy day, finding her apprehenfions in-
creafe, Mrs. Shirley, her excellent grandmother, bleffed
and encouraged her ; and Sir Charles entreated, that in
compliment to the beft of parents, fhe would refume her
ufual prefence of mind ; elfe I, faid he, who fhould glory
in receiving the honour of your hand before a thoufand
witneffes, fhall be forry that I acquiefced fo cheerfully for
a public celebration. This day, my deareft life, faid he,
we call upon the world to witnefs our mutual joy. Let
us fhew that world, that our hearts are one, and that the
facred ceremony cannot make it more fo. The engage-
ment is a holy one ; and let us fhew the multitude, as
well as our furrounding friends, that we think it a laud-
able one. I call upon you, my deareft love, to juftify my
joy by your vifible approbation. The world around you
has been accuftomed to fee your lovers, fhew them now
the hufband of your choice. Oh, Sir, returned the lady,
you have given me a motive, which through the whole
facred tranfaction I will never lofe fight of.

The ladies were all elegantly dreffed ; but Mifs Byron
was in virgin white. The proceffion to church confifted
of eight coaches and four, and the way was lined with
fpectators. On their ftopping at the church-yard, four
tenants daughters, the eldeft not above thirteen, unex-
pectedly appeared with neat bafkets in their hands, filled

K

with flowers ; and as foon as the bride, Mr. Selby, Sir Charles, and Mrs. Shirley alighted, thefe pretty little Flora's, all dreffed in white, with chaplets of flowers for head dreffes, large nofegays in their bofoms, white ribbons adorning their ftays and their bafkets, fome ftreaming down, and others tied round the handles in true lovers knots, attended the company, two going before, and the others here and there, all ftrewing flowers.

At the conclufion of the ceremony, Sir Charles, with a joy that lighted up a finer flufh than ufual in his face, took the bride by the hand, and faluting her, faid in an audible voice, May God, my deareft life, be gracious to your Grandifon, as he will be good to his Harriet, now no longer Byron ! She courtefied low, every one blefling her, and pronouncing her the lovelieft of women, and him the politeft and moft graceful of men. Sir Charles now led her into the veftry, followed by the reft of their friends ; and the moment fhe beheld her grandmother, fhe kneeling, cried, Blefs, madam, your happy, happy child. God forever blefs, faid fhe, the darling of my heart ! Sir Charles then, bending his knee to the venerable lady, faid, Receive and blefs alfo your fon. The good lady was affected ; fhe flid off her feat on her knees, and lifting up her hands and eyes, while the tears trickled down her cheeks, cried, Thou Almighty, blefs the dear fon of my wifhes ! He raifed her with a pious tendernefs, and faluted her, Excellent lady ! faid he ; but was too much affected to fay more ; and having feated her, turned to Mrs. Selby. Words are poor, faid he. My actions, my behaviour fhall fpeak the grateful fenfe I have of your goodnefs, faluting her ; of yours, madam, to Mrs. Shirley ; and of yours, my deareft life, addref-

fing himfelf again to his lovely bride, who feemed fcarce
able to fupport her joy.   Let me once more, added he,
blefs the hand that has bleffed me ! She cheerfully offered it.   I give you, Sir, faid fhe, my hand, courtefying, and
with it a poor but grateful heart—It is all your own. He
bowed upon it, unable to fpeak.   Joy, joy, joy, was wifhed the happy pair from every mouth.   See, my dear
young ladies, faid the happy and inftruftive Mrs. Shirley,
addreffing herfelf to feveral who had entered the veftry,
the reward of duty, virtue, and obedience ! How unhappy muft thofe parents and relations be, whofe daughters,
unlike our Harriet, have difgraced themfelves and their
families by a fhameful choice ! As my Harriet's is, fuch,
looking round her, be your lot, my amiable daughters !
They each befought her hand, kiffed it, and promifed to
cherifh the memory of what they had feen and heard.

The moment the ceremony was concluded, the bells
were fet a ringing, and Sir Charles led his lovely bride
through a lane of applauding fpeftators, in the church
and church-yard, flowers being ftill ftrewed as they paffed, by little Flora's.   My fweet girls, faid he, I defire
you to complete the honour you have done us by giving
us your company at Selby-houfe.   They came back in
the fame order they went, and on their affembling in the
great hall, mutual congratulations flowed from every
mouth :   every man faluted the happy bride, and the
equally happy bridegroom faluted every lady.   The lady
G—, Sir Charles's fifter, led her into a parlour, and
holding her in her arms, Now, my dear, faid fhe, do I
falute my real fifter, my fifter Grandifon, both in Lady
L———'s name and my own : May God confirm and
eftablifh your happinefs ! My deareft, deareft lady

G——, returned the bride, how grateful, how encouraging
is your kind falutation ! Your continued love, and that
of my dear lady L——, will be effential to my happinefs !
But why, ladies, faid Sir Charles, do you fequefter yourfelves from the company ? Are we not all of a family
to-day ? The four little Flora's with their bafkets in
their hands are entering the gates : we will join the company, and call them in.   They returned into the great
hall, and the pretty Flora's being introduced, Sir Charles
taking each by the hand, faid, My pretty loves, I wifh I
could prefent you with as pretty flowers as you threw
away in honour of this company, putting five guineas into each bafket ; and then prefented them, two in each
hand, to his bride, who received them with the moft
graceful familiarity and eafe.

Afterwards the children defiring to return to their parents, were conducted to them ; but foon came back with
a requeft from all the tenants, for whom an entertainment
had been provided in the leffer park, that fome time in the
day, they might have the honour of feeing the bridegroom and bride among them, were it only for two minutes ; but this the bride declining, Sir Charles promifed
to go and make her excufe.

In the afternoon Sir Charles went, agreeable to his
promife, when the tenants and their wives all wifhed him
joy ; and as they would not fit down while he ftood, he
took his feat, and the reft followed his example.   One of
the honeft men obferved, that he remembered the marriage of Mr. and Mrs. Byron, and praifed them as the
beft and happieft of mankind.   Another remembered the
birth of the bride ; and others talked of what an excellent lady fhe was from her infancy.   And let me tell you,

K 2 -

Sir, faid a grey-headed man, that you will have much
ado to deferve her.   Sir Charles was highly pleafed with
his honeft freedom : he apologized for his not bringing her
with him ; but told them that he hoped they fhould have
one happy dinner together, before he left Northamton-
fhire ; and then, with his ufual affability, eafe, and politenefs, took his leave.   The happy day was concluded
with a ball, which was opened by the bride and bridegroom, by the defire of the whole company.

Sir Charles wrote the very next day to inform his
dear friend the Barone della Porretta of the actual celebration of his nuptials, and concluded with a caution,
given in the warmeft terms, againft urging Clementina
with two much earneftnefs to marry.   The fame day, by
Sir Charles's defire, the church-wardens brought a lift of
the poor, amounting to upwards of a hundred and forty
perfons, divided into two claffes ; the one of the acknow-
ledged poor, the other of houfe-keepers and labouring
people, who were afhamed to apply, but to whom the
church-wardens knew his bounty would be acceptable.
He gave very liberally ; and in particular, to about thirty
of the laft he gave very handfomely ; and the church-
wardens, who were men of great humanity, went away
bleffing him.

On the following Sunday, the relations of the bride
and bridegroom were all richly dreffed.   The bride, lovely
in any drefs, wore richer filks than ufual, coftly laces,
and jewels that added grace to that admirable proportion,
and thofe fine features, to which no painter has ever been
able to do juftice.   The bridegroom was principally admired for his native eafe and dignity, and that inatten-
tion to his own appearance, which fhews the truly fine

gentleman, accuftomed to be always elegant. On his
lady's coming to him and her friends, they involuntarily
rofe as if to pay her homage ; but Sir Charles approach-
ing her with an air of unufual freedom, cried, How lovely ! But what is even all this amazing lovelinefs to the
graces of her mind ? They every hour rife upon me.
She hardly opens her lips, but I find reafon to blefs God
and you, my dear ladies, bowing to Mrs. Shirley and
Mrs. Selby ; for God and you have given her goodnefs.
My dear life, allow me to fay, that this perfon, which
will be your firft perfection in every ftranger's eye, is but
a fecond in mine. Teach me, Sir, faid fhe, to deferve
your love, by improving the mind you have the goodnefs
to prefer, and then I fhall be the happieft of women upon
earth. The church was extremely crouded, and the
charming couple greatly admired ; Sir Charles and his
bride, however, did not forget that humble deportment
due to the place, which feemed to render them abfent for
the time from that fplendor which attracted every eye
out of the pews in which the family were placed. The
church, in the afternoon, was ftill more crouded. How
was Sir Charles bleffed by the poor, and people of low
circumftances, for his well-difpofed bounty ! Sir Charles
and his bride, having received and returned the vifits of
the neighbouring gentry, and given the tenants their
company at another entertainment provided for them,
they fet out for Grandifon-hall, Sir Charles's principal
feat ; where having again run the round of receiving and
paying vifits, they fettled into that pleafing ferenity, that
conftitutes the moft perfect ftate of human happinefs.

A confiderable part of his time was now employed in
improving his eftate, in order to enable him to exercife

his generous spirit. He became acquainted with every tenant, and even cottager, enquiring into their circumstances, the number of their children, and their prospects. When they were distressed, he would forgive arrears of rent, or send them on urgent occasions a supply of money ; and when they had no prospect of success, he gave them money to quit. At the tenant's desire, he transplanted one to a larger farm, and another to a less, according to their stock, or the probability of success. By these means, his tenants overcame every difficulty, and grew rich, while he himself reaped the benefit of his own generosity, by the ease and punctuality with which they paid their rents. On the other hand, he began to employ himself, in reconciling the differences between his friends. and tenants ; and frequently united those, who from any misunderstanding became at variance ; it being his settled opinion, that a day spent in restoring peace and harmony, let the objects be ever so mean, is more pleasing, upon reflection, than a day spent in the most elegant indulgence.

CHAP. XIII.

Clementina, who had escaped from her friends, came to England to avoid marrying the Count of Belvedere, and is protected by Sir Charles and his Lady. She is followed by her Relations and Friends, who were received by Sir Charles, and by his Managemement every Uneasiness is removed. The Conclusion.

WHILE Sir Charles was thus employed in the generous acts of humanity and friendship, a letter they received from the Barone della Porretta filled him with deep concern. By this letter he learned, that the Lady Clementina being strongly bent on taking the veil, had been pressed with such earnestness and incessant importunity to give her hand to the Count of Belvedere, as had greatly disordered her brain, and that, to avoid that union, and put a stop to these importunate solicitations, she had fled from her friends, and with no other attendants than her page, an English youth, and her servant Laura, had embarked in a vessel bound for London ; and that both her father, mother, and himself, together with several other of her friends, being inconsolable for her loss, were following her ; beseeching him to search for the fugitive Clementina, and to provide them lodgings against their arrival. It is no wonder that this news gave both Sir Charles and his lady great concern. They were then at Grandison-hall, and that lady being firmly convinced of the steadiness of his virtue, immediately persuaded him to give the unhappy Clementina his pro-

tection. Dear Sir, faid fhe, confider me as a ftrength-
ener, not as a weakener of your hands, in her fervice.
My only anxiety is for her fafety and honour, and for
your concern on the affecting occafion, and let me by
fympathizing with you, leffen it. Soul of my foul, cried
he, clafping her to his bofom, I had not the leaft doubt
of your generous goodnefs. It would be doing injuftice
to the unhappy lady, and to the knowledge I have of my
own heart, as well as to you, the abfolute miftrefs of it,
to think it neceffary to make profeffions of my inviolable
love to you. I will acquaint you with every ftep I take
on this occafion, and muft have your advice as I go
along ; for fuch delicate minds as yours and Clementina's muft be nearly allied.

Sir Charles immediately rode poft to town, where he
found a long letter from the fugitive lady, who, in un-
connected ramblings, lamented the ftep fhe had taken ;
obferving, that fhe was far from being happy, but wifhed
for his advice and protection, though fhe did not dare to
let him know where he might fee her ; yet at the fame
time informed him how he might direct a letter fo as to
come to her hands. He ftrove, in his anfwer, to footh
her mind ; offering to put her under his lady's or his
fifter's protection ; and befeeching her to remove his
anxiety, by giving him an immediate opportunity of feeing her. In another letter, fhe earneftly endeavoured to
engage him to ufe his intereft with her friends, to allow
her the freedom of her choice, and prevent her being for-
ced to marry the Count of Belvedere. All this he readily
promifed in his reply ; and fhe allowed him to wait on her.

Sir Charles went, and was introduced by her fervant
Laura. On his entering the room, he immediately wel-

comed her to England. Do you, can you, cried fhe, bid
me welcome, me a fugitive, an ingrate, undutiful !—O
Chevalier, don't debafe your unfullied character, by ap-
proving the unnatural ftep I have taken. I do bid you
welcome, madam, faid he ; your brother, your friend,
from his foul, welcomes you to England. Let me know,
Chevalier, before another word paffes, returned fhe,
whether I have a father ? whether I have a mother ?
Thank God, madam, you have both, faid he. God, I
thank thee ! cried fhe, lifting up her hands. Had I not,
diftraction would have been my portion ! If they had
been no more, I fhould have thought myfelf the moft
deteftable of parricides. They are in the utmoft diftrefs,
rejoined he, for your fafety ; and will think themfelves
happy when they know that you are well, and in the poffeffion of your brother Grandifon. Will they, Sir ? cried
fhe ; O how ftrange ! They fo cruel, yet fo indulgent !
I fo dutiful, yet a fugitive ! But determined as I was
againft entering into a ftate I had too much honour to
enter with a reluctant heart, could I have taken any
other ftep to free myfelf from the cruelty of perfuafion ?
Your confcience, madam, faid he, is a law to you. If
that accufes you, you'll repent ; if it acquits you, who
fhall prefume to condemn ? Sir Charles then ftrove to
raife her fpirits, by expatiating on the kind reception fhe
would meet with among his friends. She then remark-
ed, that he forbore to mention the principal perfon among
them, and afked what his lady would think of the poor
fugitive Clementina ? defiring him to affure her, that
fhe would not have landed in England, if he had not been
married ; adding, that fhould fhe render him and his lady unhappy, no perfon on earth could hate her fo much

as fhe fhould hate herfelf.   Sir Charles affured her, that
her happinefs was really effential to that of them both ;
that his Harriet was another Clementina, whom fhe
muft know and love, for fhe was prepared to receive her
as the deareft of her fifters.   Generous Lady Grandifon !
faid fhe, I have heard her charaĉter, and congratulate
you, Sir, on your happinefs ; I fhould have been grieved
had you not met with a lady worthy of you : but my being fenfible of your happinefs, and that you do not blame
me for declining your addreffes, will contribute more to
my peace of mind than I can exprefs.   When I have
more courage, and this poor heart is eafed of that part of
its trouble, you fhall prefent me to her.   In the mean
time tell her, that I will love her ; and that I fhall ever
think myfelf under the higheft obligations for making
him happy, whom once, but for a fuperior motive, I had
the vanity to think I could have made fo.   She here
turned away her glowing face, bedewed with tears, while
Sir Charles's admiration of her greatnefs of mind, fo like
that of his own Harriet, kept him filent ; but he at laft
perfuaded her to accept of an apartment at Lady L——'s,
fhe confented to go thither the next day.   Sir Charles
and his fifter came the next morning, and after an affeĉt-
ing interview, took her away in Lord L's coach.   All
the ladies of Sir Charles's family ftrove who fhould
moft oblige the unhappy Clementina ; and particularly
his Lady, who had all along admired her for her virtues
and noble magnanimity, and now treated her with the
tender affeĉtion of a beloved fifter.   Clementina had not
been long acquainted with the principal perfons of this
happy family, when Sir Charles received a letter by an
exprefs from his dear friend the Barone, to let him know

the Marquis and the Marchionefs, with feveral of their
friends, were landed at Dover ; upon which he immedi-
diately fet out with four coaches and fix of his own and
his friends, to accommodate them and their attendants,
he having before fitted up his houfe in Grofvenor-fquare
for their reception. He had not been long gone, when
the Count of Belvedere, who impatiently longed to hear
news of Clementina, arrived with one of his friends, and
were received by Lady Grandifon with all poffible marks
of refpect : fhe let them know that fhe was fafe, and in
good hands ; but no arguments could prevail on her to
inform them where that lady was.

Sir Charles no fooner arrived at Dover, than he was
received with inexpreffible joy by the whole noble family ;
however, though he found them breathing nothing but
reconciliation and love to their dear Clementina, he was
determined to keep her concealed, till he was fully fatif-
fied that her underftanding could not be endangered by
her being teazed to marry the Count of Belvedere.

Sir Charles conducted the family, by eafy journies, to
London, where he brought them to the houfe he had
provided for their reception ; and was agreeably furprifed on their arrival, at finding that his lady had, unknown to him, prepared an elegant repaft. The Marchionefs was fo impatient to fee Clementina, that every
one was afraid of the confequences, with refpect to her
health ; and, on the other hand, the young lady was
grieved at finding herfelf fo fituated, as to be obliged to
caufe her parents to enter into articles with her before
fhe kneeled to them, which fhe longed to do, notwithftanding her dreading to fee them. Sir Charles, by the
defire of all parties, drew up a paper, copies of which

L

were given both to the principal perfons of her family,
and to Clementina ; in which he propofed, that fhe
fhould lay afide all thoughts of retiring to a convent, be
allowed to chufe her way of life, and her attendants ;
that her parents and brothers fhould promife never to
perfuade her, much lefs to compel her, to marry any
man ; and that the Court of Belvedere fhould difcon-
tinue his addreffes. After fome debate the whole family
confented to thefe articles ; but the Lady Clementina
found the greateft difficulty in giving up her favorite pro-
jeſt of taking the veil ; nor could the Count of Belvedere,
without the greateft agony of mind, fubmit to difcon-
tinue his pretenfions. Thefe precautions being taken,
Clementina was to be introduced to her longing parents ;
but her dread of appearing before them made her entreat
the Lady Grandifon and the Lady L—to introduce and
countenance her by their prefence ; to which they. wil-
lingly confented. At the time fixed for this affecting interview, Sir Charles went to prepare her expecting parents, while the Lady Grandifon waited upon her. Clementina looking wild and difordered, and giving Lady L—
and Lady Grandifon her hand, was led to the coach ; but
at ftepping in fhe trembled, and appeared much difturbed.
They gave her all the comfort they were able, while the
coach drove to Grofvenor-Square. On its ftopping, Sir
Charles appeared, and feeing her emotion, It is kind, my
dear fifter, faid he, to accompany the Lady Clementina—Your goodnefs will be rewarded by the pleafure of
feeing the moft gracious reception that ever indulgent
parents gave a long abfent daughter. O Chevalier !
was all Clementina could fay. He then told her that he
would lead her into a drawing-room, where fhe fhould
fee none but thofe who were with her. Vifibly encoura-

ged, fhe gave him her trembling hand, and he led her in,
followed by the two ladies, who feated themfelves on each
fide of her, but with difficulty kept her from fainting by
their falts and foothing : on her recovering a little, holding up her finger with wildnefs in her looks, fhe caft her
eyes to the doors and windows, crying, Hufh ! they will
hear us ; but foon coming more to herfelf, O Chevalier !
faid fhe, what fhall I fay ? How fhall I look ? What
fhall I do ? Am I indeed in the fame houfe with my father, my mother, Jeronymo ? Who elfe ? who elfe ?
My deareft Clementina, faid Sir Charles, it is, from love
and tendernefs to you, agreed, that you firft only fee your
mother, then your father, and at your own pleafure your
brothers, Mrs. Beaumont, and Father Marefcotti.
Your Mamma, madam, who is all indulgence, is impatient to hold you to her heart. What joy will you give
her ! He offered his hand, and fhe gave him hers, making a motion for the two ladies to come with her, and
who followed her into the room, where was her expecting
mother. They ran to each other with open arms. O
my Clementina ! O my mamma ! was all they cold utter : they funk on the floor, the mother's arms about the
daughter's neck, the daughters's about the mother's waift.
Sir Charles lifting them up, feated them by each other.
Pardon ! pardon ! pardon !, cried Clementina, lifting
up her hands and eyes, and fliding out of her mother's
arms on her knees. The Marquis, unable longer to
contain himfelf, rufhed in, crying, My daughter ! my
child ! My Clementina ! do I once more fee my child ?
Sir Charles had lifted her up, when her father entered,
but fhe again funk down proftrate on the floor, with her
arms extended, crying, O father, forgive ! forgive me,

O my father ! By Sir Charles's affistance he raifed her up, and feating her between himfelf and his lady, they both threw their arms about her ; fhe in broken accents repeating prayers for forgivenefs, while they in accents as broken, uttered their bleffings.

When Clementina's firft emotions were over, and fhe began to look up, fhe cried, Behold, madam, behold, my Lord, looking at Lady L——, the hofpitable lady with whom I have lived. Behold, looking at Lady Grandi-fon, a more than woman, an angel !—She here feemed at a lofs for words. We have before, faid the Marquis, feen and admired, in Lady Grandifon, the nobleft of all women. He arofe to approach the ladies, when Sir Charles leading them both to him, Clementina firft fnatched Lady Grandifon's hand, and eagerly preffed it to her lips, and then Lady L——'s. Her heart was full, and fhe feemed unable to fpeak ; when the two ladies, with their eyes over-flowing with tears, congratulated the father, mother, and daughter.

Sir Charles then withdrew, but foon returned with the Bifhop and Seignior Jeronymo. It is not eafy to deter-mine whether thefe Lords fhewed more joy than Clem-entina did fhame and confufion. She attempted to beg pardon, but the Bifhop cried, Not one word of paft afflic-tions. None are in fault. We are all once more hap-py ; happy by means of this friend of mankind in gene-ral, and of our family in particular. My ever noble and venerable brother, faid Jeronymo, who had clafped his fifter to his fond heart, how I love you for thus comfort-ing and encouraging the dear Clementina ! Every arti-cle of my Grandifon's propofals fhall be carried into exe-cution. We will, as he has defired, rejoice with him in

England; and he, and all thofe who are dear to him, fhall accompany us to Italy.   Sir Charles then introdu-ced the juftly efteemed Mrs. Beaumont, when Clemen-tina throwing herfelf into her arms, cried, Forgive me, virtue will ! Pardon her who never, never would have fo difgraced your excellent leffons, and her mamma's bright example, had not her unhappy mind been darken-ed by a heavy cloud.   My dear Lady, returned fhe, it was not your fault, but your misfortune.   You deferved pity and not blame.   We all think fo, and came here to heal your wounded mind : be that healed, and we all fhall be happy.

The articles, figned and witneffed, were put into her hands a day or two after; when having written her name, fhe tore off the other names, and kiffing the torn bit, put it in her bofom ; then falling herfelf on her knees to her father and mother, who ftood together, fhe prefented the paper, crying, Never let it be mentioned that your Clem-entina has prefumed to bind by thefe articles the deareft of parents.   My name ftands, and will be a witnefs againft me, if I break thofe I have figned ; but in your forgive-nefs, my Lord, in yours, madam, and in a thoufand acts of indulgence, I have too much experienced your paft goodnefs to doubt the future.   May God enable your Clementina to be all you wifh !   Only indulge me in my choice of a fingle life, and your word is all the affurance I defire.   They embraced her ; then tenderly raifing her, embraced her again.

This noble lady was not informed till the day before, that the Count of Belvedere had accompanied her friends to England.   Sir Charles made ufe of great precaution in telling her ; and at the fame time let her know that the

Count was very defirous of taking his leave of her. She confented to fee him as one of the friends of her father and brothers, and in that light deferred his departure. She had afterwards feveral converfations with him, and before all her relations behaved towards him with the refpect due to his merit. She was fenfible of the ardour with which her parents and brothers wifhed to fee her married to that accomplifhed nobleman. She could not help obferving the pleafure that fparkled in his eyes whenever fhe was pleafed to enter into difcourfe with him ; and ferioufly confidering their motives, with the extraordinary merit of the Count, together with the reafons that had induced her to refolve never to enter into the marriage ftate, fhe, at length, began to hefitate, and voluntarily promifed her relations, that if within a year's time fhe fhould find no reafon to change her mind, fhe would cheerfully comply with their wifhes.

In fhort, this noble family ftaid feveral months with Sir Charles, part of which time they paffed at Grandifon-Hall. Every opportunity was taken to render their refidence in England as agreeable as poffible, and on their taking their leave, Sir Charles and his Lady attended them to Dover. Jeronymo, however, ftaid in England with Sir Charles, in order to reap the benefit of the Bath waters, by means of which, added to the affiftance he had received from the excellent Mr. Lowther, he was perfectly recovered.

The next year, Sir Charles and his Lady, with his two fifters and their Lords, attended him to Italy, where they were received by his noble family with tranfports of joy. They had there the pleafure to find the lady Clementina perfectly free from her unhappy diforder of mind, by whieh fhe had been fo long afflicted. After having fpent feveral months in Italy, Sir Charles and his Lady, in company with his brothers and fifters, returned together to England, where they had the pleafure to refume their former plan of life. Their piety and virtue are the four-ces of the nobleft pleafures that can fill the human mind. While they are admired and beloved by their friends, they are regarded with grateful affection by their tenants, and reverenced by the poor.

F I N I S.

THE Royal Convert, or the Force of Truth ; being a wonderful and ftrange Relation of the Converfion of *Varanes,* Prince of Perfia, and two young Ladies, to the Chriftian Faith ; their Trials and Sufferings on that Account ; of the ftrange Death of one of the Ladies, and of the Prince's Succefs over his enemies, and converting at laft his cruel Father, and his whole Kingdom. Written in French by the Meffieurs of Port-Royal, and now newly tranflated into Englifh.

The French Convert ; being a True Relation of the Happy Converfion of a Noble French Lady, from the Errors and Superftitions of Popery, to the Reformed Religion, by Means of a Proteftant Gardener, her Servant. Wherein are fhewed, her great and unparallelled Sufferings on Account of her faid Converfion ; her wonderful Deliverance from two Affaffins, hired by a Popifh Prieft to murder her ; her miraculous Prefervation in a Wood for two Years, and the providential Manner of her being found by her Hufband, who, together with her Parents, was brought over, by her Means, to

to the true Religion, as were alſo divers others. The whole Relation was ſent by a Pro-
teſtant Miniſter, a Priſoner in France, to a
French Refugee in London. To which is
added, A ſhort Account of Popiſh Cruelty
Ireland.

The Life, Travels and Adventures
of Edward Wortley Montague, Eſq. ſon to
the moſt famous Traveller, Lady Mary Montague ; exhibiting his very extraordinary
tranſactions in England, France, Italy, Tur-
key, Arabia, Egypt, and the Holy Land ;
with Remarks on the Manners and Cuſtoms
of the Oriental World.

The Holy Bible abridged ; or, the
Hiſtory of the Old and New-Teſtament—il-
luſtrated with Notes, and adorned with 60
Pictures, containing lively repreſentations of
the moſt remarkable events and tranſactions,
recorded in the ſacred Scriptures.

A Token for Children, being an
exact Account of the Converſion, holy and
exemplary Lives and joyful Death of ſeveral
young Children. By James Janeway, miniſter of the Goſpel.—To which is added, a
Token for the Children of New-England,
or, ſome Examples of Children, in whom
the Fear of God was remarkably budding
before they died, in ſeveral parts of New-

England. Preferved and publifhed for the encouragement of piety in other Children. With additions.

A fhort and eafy Guide to Arith-metick, containing all that is neceffary to tranfact common Bufinefs.—Very fuitable all thofe who wifh to learn only the moft ufeful parts of that neceffary fcience.

An approved Collection of enter-taining Stories, calculated for the Inftruction and Amufement of all little Mafters and Miffes. By Solomon Winlove, Efq.

The Adventures of Capt. Gulliver, in a Voyage to the Iflands of Lilliput and Brobdingnag. Adorned with Cuts.

The Hiftory of Sinbad the Sailor; containing an Account of his feveral furpriz-ing Voyages, and miraculous Efcapes.

Mr. Hervey's Treatife on the re ligious Education of Daughters.

Doctor Martinett's Catechifm of Nature.